St Elizabeth's Children's Hospital London

Dealing with sick kids can be heartbreaking, funny, and uplifting, often all at once!

This series takes a look at a hospital set up especially to deal with such children, peeping behind the scenes into almost all the departments and clinics, exploring the problems and solutions of various diseases, while watching the staff fall helplessly in love—with the kids and with each other.

Enjoy!

As a person who lists her hobbies as reading, reading and reading, it is hardly surprising **Meredith Webber** fell into writing when she needed a job she could do at home. Not that anyone in the family considers it a 'real job'! She is fortunate enough to live on the Gold Coast in Queensland, Australia, as this gives her the opportunity to catch up with many other people with the same 'unreal' job when they visit the popular tourist area.

Recent titles by the same author:

WEDDING BELLS

MEREDITH WEBBER

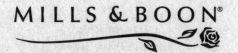
MILLS & BOON®

First published in Great Britain 2000
Harlequin Mills & Boon Limited,
Eton House, 18-24 Paradise Road, Richmond, Surrey TW9 1SR

© Meredith Webber 2000

ISBN 0 263 82443 8

Set in Times Roman 10½ on 11½ pt.
112-0108-50830

Printed and bound in Spain
by Litografia Rosés S.A., Barcelona

CHAPTER ONE

GHOSTS of the thousands of children who had visited the St Elizabeth's Children's Hospital accompanied William as he walked through the deserted and dimly lit outpatients department. Echoes of tears and laughter, shadows of pain and despair.

He shrugged his shoulders to throw off the fancy. He was a man of science, not fantasy, a pragmatist through and through, despite what Isobel had told him.

And why would Isobel suddenly pop up in his head after—what? Six months?

He pushed open the door to the suite of rooms housing the paediatric rheumatology unit and snapped on the light.

'That should settle the ghosts,' he said to the vacant chairs in the small reception area. 'All of them,' he added firmly, crossing to the office he'd be sharing, on a temporary basis, with two regular members of the unit staff.

He opened the door, and felt the hairs on the back of his neck crawl to attention. The sense of another presence was so strong he ducked back instinctively, although a flimsy internal door wouldn't be much protection against a bullet.

Not that one came zinging over his head.

Nor did a knife-wielding madman come flying out.

In fact, nothing happened, and, after a second as long as an hour had ticked by, he straightened cautiously, his body tense, every sense alert for a further indication that an intruder was in the room, every muscle on stand-by for fight or flight.

He was berating himself for an overactive imagination

when he heard a soft snuffling sound—halfway between a deep breath and a gentle snore.

Relief that he hadn't imagined an intruder eased a little of his tension, but he was still wary. It seemed unlikely that either of the women with whom he'd share this office would be using it as overnight accommodation.

The phrase, 'Who's been sleeping in my office chair?' echoed irrelevantly in his head, and was countered by a firm, 'Get serious' from the no-nonsense persona within him.

Hospital security was good these days but who knew when some drug-crazed unfortunate would get lucky and find a way in? He reached around the door jamb and felt for a light switch.

'Wrong door, and definitely the wrong fairy tale,' he muttered to himself as the light snapped on to reveal, not the office he'd expected, but one of the small therapy rooms. And on the table in the centre, unperturbed by either the light or any sense of his presence, was a woman.

She lay on her back, eyes closed but lips slightly parted, hands clasped beneath the slight swell of her breasts, feet neatly aligned.

William stepped gingerly forward and peered more closely. He knew immediately she wasn't Sleeping Beauty because she wore a short white coat and SB, as far as he could recall, hadn't chosen medicine as a career.

Nor would SB have sported a clutter of tiny pale freckles across the bridge of her nose. Eleven of them, to be exact.

Why are you standing there counting this woman's freckles? his sensible self demanded, but he ignored it, as he seemed to be doing with increasing frequency these days, and continued his observations.

Apart from the freckles, her skin had the clear translucence so admired as 'an English complexion'. Its paleness was accentuated by the short dark hair, at the moment sticking out every which way, that framed her face. Dark eyebrows arced delicately above her eyes, black feathery eyelashes rested on skin bruised to a grey-blue colour by lack of sleep.

The freckled nose was what could only be called pert. It started out short and straight, but had a small point to its tip—not quite tilting upward, but perhaps considering going that way. He guessed she hated it. Someone who could sleep so tidily probably considered herself sensible and practical—but that nose killed the image.

As did the lips. The shapely upper one was slightly fuller than the lower, and was lifted enough to reveal the tips of two white teeth, while the lower one was softly sensuous. Both were a soft pink—nipple pink, he guessed they'd call it on a colour chart—rimmed by a whitish line that defined their shape and beauty.

Vermilion border. The computer in his brain threw up the medical term for human lips, while the irreverent voice offered other suggestions about lips and sleeping beauties.

Which reminded him that this was voyeurism and he should remove himself from her vicinity. Find the right door, his desk, and the pile of files Annette had said she'd leave out for him. He'd come in early, even forgoing his morning run, to read up on the patients he'd be treating this first day. He needed to know something about them!

His feet failed to move on cue, something going haywire in the communication links between them and his head. Quite possible, when you considered there were at least six feet of nerve fibres through which the messages had to travel.

Now, he told them, but they remained obdurate, as if listening to his eyes, which were still absorbing the image of the sleeping woman, not the orders of his brain.

She was too pale, but her body, beneath the white coat and the neat shirt and skirt she wore under it, seemed well put together, neither too thin nor too fat, yet with an air of…Fragility?

All bodies were fragile, he reminded himself. More so than most people realised.

The tiny sound she made, a second muffled kind of snore, snapped him out of his silent observation and sent him stepping gingerly backwards. Should he switch off the light? Let her sleep?

A quick glance at the clock above the door told him she couldn't stay much longer. In half an hour, he guessed, staff would start arriving. In less than an hour, he'd need the table himself to treat his first patient.

Coffee!

He'd been shown the new coffee-maker purchased for the therapy office, and the cupboard with emergency rations of tea, ground coffee and biscuits. If he left this door open, and the office door, the smell of brewing coffee would permeate through all the rooms and perhaps infiltrate the senses of his sleeping beauty, waking her as gently as a kiss.

He left the room before the bit of himself he could never quite repress got any more ideas.

Prue dreamt of coffee, and images of sticky buns made her stomach gurgle in anticipation. A late-night snack in the staff room during her houseman years. Paul, impossibly handsome, teasing her for a kiss. Her lips puckered to meet his, her arms reached out to enfold his slim, elegant body.

But as she moved to hold him she felt herself falling, down into that bottomless hole of sleep. She sat up with a jerk, hands clutching at the edge of the treatment table when she realised the falling part was real enough.

The light was on, coffee brewing somewhere—no wonder it had sneaked into her dream. Time? What was the time? Had the entire unit staff arrived and found her kipping on the treatment table?

Why hadn't someone woken her?

She dropped down to the floor, slipped on her shoes, and headed towards the smell of coffee.

'Why didn't you wake me?' she demanded, pushing open the door to the therapists' office and marching in, expecting to see Pat or Annette. Crystal was never early.

'I debated it and decided anyone who could sleep so soundly on a narrow and uncomfortable treatment table must need all the rest she could get. In the meantime, you were warming it nicely for my first patient.'

The man who delivered this quite logical explanation was a total stranger, and, apart from a quick look over his shoulder as she'd entered the room, he'd remained with his back to her, fussing over the coffee-pot.

Now he turned and she barely had time to register an impressive height and healthy solidity before he smiled and registering anything became difficult.

'I ducked out to Dunwoody and bought sticky buns, thinking you might need more sustenance than biscuits,' he told her. 'Do you like sticky buns?'

Prue stared at him, unable to put together a reply as the collision of her dream of sticky buns and her reaction to this stranger jammed all her thought processes.

'Who are you?' she asked, belatedly running a hand across her short cropped hair in the hope it didn't look quite as bad as she feared it would.

'That was to be my next question,' he replied, then he smiled again. 'Well, actually, I was going to ask about milk and sugar and repeat the sticky bun bit first. Then ask who you are and whether it's a back problem that makes you seek out uncomfortable beds.'

His voice was light for such a big man, a tenor rather than a bass, but with a clean, beautiful pitch that carried it deep into her body. She knew she should be answering questions, not thinking of this man's voice, but the dream must have stayed with her, leaving reality a little fuzzy—thought processes difficult.

Perhaps if she washed her face, splashed a bit of cold water around, stuck her head under a tap.

Although she suspected the head wouldn't be enough, she'd probably need to stick her whole body under a tap.

'Excuse me,' she muttered, and headed for the unit washrooms where one glance in the mirror confirmed her fears about her hair, while the wide blue eyes staring back at her suggested she was looking as dull-witted as she felt.

She'd had a shower and changed into clean underwear in a lull somewhere around midnight, but sleeping in her clothes always made her feel sticky and uncomfortable.

Shrugging off her coat, she washed her face and arms, scrubbing her hands across her skin, and scooping water onto her head and neck in an effort to startle her brain back into working order.

The paper towels fell into pieces as she tried to dry herself, and she then had to pick small scraps of damp paper off her nose and cheeks. She felt in her pocket for a comb. No such luck! It was in her handbag in the locker in the doctors' mess. She'd been called down to A and E, then had sneaked in here as soon as the patient had been transferred to Neurology.

She finger-combed her wet hair into a semblance of order, wondering why snatching a quick hour's sleep on a treatment table had seemed such a good idea at the time.

'I have a morning clinic here so thought I should be on hand.' She answered her own question out loud as she cautiously re-entered the therapists' office and found the man had poured coffee and put the jar of sugar and a carton of milk beside one of the beakers.

'Much better than falling asleep somewhere else, then wondering where you're supposed to be next,' he agreed, as if he'd been through the years of sleep deprivation most young doctors suffered. 'I'm William Alexander, by the way. Filling in for Annette while she's on leave.'

The water must have helped, for Prue's brain worked quite well accepting this information. Believing it was something else.

'You're a physio?' she asked, reassessing the tall, powerful frame—well, that figured—the intelligent-looking head topped with dark red-brown hair, and the deep, all-seeing dark eyes.

'Something wrong with being a physio?' he asked mildly.

It was the glasses that were throwing her, she decided. He must have put them on to read something while she was out of the room. He looked more like an academic—a geek—than a man of action. Although a very good-looking geek. Quite exceptionally good-looking, in fact. Not to mention sexy!

'No,' she managed to reply, cutting short these mental qualifications. 'No. Annette's just smaller, and she's a—'

She stopped abruptly, wondering for the hundredth time if too little sleep was worse than none at all. So she'd feel better later! So what!

'Woman,' he finished for her, smiling in the kindly way indulgent parents smiled at childish folly. 'Like doctors, physios come in a range of race, creed, size, colour and sex.'

The final word startled her out of thoughts of how his smile released the impression of academia—but enhanced the good looks.

'I'm Prue Valentine,' she said, realising she'd better change the subject before she sank any deeper into conversational quicksands. 'I'm working under Mark Gregory, the rheumatology consultant, but, as this is a separate unit without a ward, I'm considered a kind of junior dogsbody as far as my hospital appointment is concerned and do normal duty in various wards. I've just started a rotation on General Medical and was on call last night. Then I've a clinic with Mark this morning which is why I decided if I was going to fall asleep anywhere, it had better be here.'

She hoped her explanation made sense to him. It seemed, to her, a little garbled.

He nodded, as if accepting it without question, and waved his hand towards the coffee.

'Help yourself to milk and sugar.'

She sank into the visitors' chair across the desk from him and reached out for the coffee. Normally she weakened it with milk, but the way her brain was behaving this morning she'd be better off with the straight caffeine.

'And are you wisely cautious?' he asked as he settled himself in the chair opposite her. 'Or is it cautiously wise?'

Prue stared at him. He'd taken off the glasses again, and she could see his eyes, a deep, dark brown, fixed enquiringly upon her.

'Isn't that what Prudence means? Or are you not a Prudence—just a Prue?'

The voice made her name, much loathed for the wisecracks she'd suffered from teachers, and the inevitable nickname of Prune, sound special.

Although she could hardly tell him as much.

'I'm too tired to be wise or cautious this morning,' she told him instead, and saw his eyebrows contract to crease two frown lines in his skin.

'You're probably grossly unfit. The medical profession is forever preaching reasonable levels of fitness to patients but very few individual practitioners are doing anything positive to improve their own health. How much exercise do you do?'

'I walk hundreds of miles a day,' Prue informed him, her lofty tone intended to put him in his place.

Not that it worked.

'Ignoring the "hundreds" which is, without doubt, a gross exaggeration, may I ask if this is as exercise or in the course of your work?'

'When I'm working. Going from ward to ward, down to A and E, to this unit, back to the ward,' she admitted, then added belligerently, 'It's still exercise.'

'Rubbish! As well as burning off fat and strengthening your bones and muscles, exercise increases your lung capacity so you can draw more air into your lungs, and provide more oxygen for your bloodstream. Whatever air there is in hospital corridors is cooled or warmed, circulated and recirculated, as artificial as candyfloss and about as useful to your health.'

Prue stared at him in disbelief.

'What are you? Some kind of exercise fanatic? Out to save the world with added oxygen? Couldn't we just wear little tanks and take what we need for our bloodstream? Or have a quick suck every now and then, as the students do to cure their hangovers.'

He shot her a scathing look and continued his dissertation on the benefits of a good lung capacity.

Prue tuned out, and took the opportunity to study him more closely. He certainly didn't look like the muscle-bound young men she'd seen on her rare visits to a gym, nor even like the bulky rugby-playing doctors who spent their off-duty time pummelling each other into the ground or kicking footballs from one end of a field to the other. He was leaner, yet solid—

She told herself his physical attributes had nothing to do with the conversation and stopped the assessment.

'I suppose, as a physio, you have to keep reasonably fit.' After all, he was good-looking enough to treat kindly, even if he was a bit ratty about exercise.

'There!' He pounced on her admission! 'You made that

statement as if being fit is an aberration. Proof of the point I'm trying to make.'

Bemused by his response, she took another sip of coffee, then eyed him warily.

'Which is?'

He sighed in much the same way her teachers used to sigh when she'd been unable to grasp the point *they* had been making.

'Lack of fitness in the medical profession.'

'Well, I'm only a very minor percentage—minimal, in fact—of said profession, so my getting fit wouldn't help much.'

'That's just where you're wrong,' he told her. 'What size shoes do you wear?'

'What size?' Prue echoed, feeling neither wise nor cautious. In fact, she felt uneasy enough to consider how stupid it was to have taken this man's word that he belonged here. He was obviously a nutter—

'Shoes!' he said impatiently. 'You'll need something to give your feet some support when we run at lunch-time. Perhaps a track suit as well. Ten or twelve, I'd say. I'll get a twelve and if it's a bit baggy it won't matter but correctly fitting shoes are important.'

Prue set her coffee-cup carefully down on the desk. If she got up and walked away—even if she ran—he'd catch up with her—catch her?—in no time. Perhaps if she humoured him.

Pat should be here soon—and Annette—although maybe the part about his taking Annette's place was true...

'Seven. I take a seven, but I really don't need running shoes. I have some at home. I'll bring them tomorrow. We can run then.'

The brown eyes twinkled at her.

'Come on too strong, haven't I?' the man called William

Alexander said ruefully. 'I'm not mad, though I do have a tendency to get swept away with my own enthusiasm.'

He smiled at her, and whatever she'd been thinking was erased from her mind.

'Not that self-knowledge puts a brake on my determination,' he added. 'I'll organise a selection of shoes and we'll run at lunch-time.'

'No way!' She held up her hands in a 'stop right there' gesture. 'This part of "we" is going to find something more comfortable than a treatment table and grab some more sleep at lunch-time,' Prue told him, valiantly resisting the alluring effects of another smile.

'For forty minutes? You'll wake up feeling fuzzy and disoriented—far worse than if you'd had no sleep at all. No, you'll see. Running's definitely better. I'll check in with you later.'

And on that note he pulled a pile of patient files towards him, bent his head, and proceeded to read through them—speed read, if the rate of his page turning was any indication.

Prue bit into her sticky bun, and sipped her coffee. Mad he might be, but he made a great cup of coffee.

And at least he wasn't fanatical enough about this good health stuff to have bought her carrot sticks for breakfast.

She leant back in the chair, bun in one hand, beaker in the other, and studied him.

William Alexander.

The name rang no bells at all, although she'd met a number of the physiotherapists at various times. Most of them were young, first or second year out of university. Working in the hospital for experience before going into private practice—or getting married and taking part-time positions as they juggled the demands of a husband, kids and a career.

She shuddered at the thought, pleased she'd finally decided about the path her life would take.

'So, what can you tell me about Ross Finch?'

The image of her career-woman self, confident, alert, all-knowing, vanished instantly, and her often-confused real self repeated the name as her brain scrabbled for something intelligent to say.

'SLE?' she said hopefully. 'Little chap, about five or six. Systemic lupus erythematosus diagnosed at three which was unusual, as it's more common in older children and also more common in girls. I think there's a family history. That him?'

Her questioner nodded, then the two vertical lines appeared again in his forehead.

'He comes in monthly?'

Prue visualised the little boy, huge brown eyes in a face thinned by illness, skin the colour of pale chocolate, marred by the thick plaques of the rash that was sometimes symptomatic of the disease.

'For blood and urine tests. It's a precaution Mark takes with all patients when steroids are tapered off. If I remember rightly, Ross had a bad flare some time ago, with inflammation in the brain which caused seizures.'

'Very good!' William Alexander said, flicking through the notes, then glancing up to bestow one of his devastating smiles on her.

Rattled by the smile, Prue retaliated with crossness.

'Was it a test? Do I get a mark? And how about an extra tick for good behaviour?'

'Only if you run with me at lunch time,' he said gravely, although she suspected it was a smile-muscle she saw twitching slightly in his cheek.

She was about to give up on humouring and tell him off, when Mark Gregory gave a perfunctory knock on the door and came charging into the room.

'Here already? Old habits die hard, eh, Will? Good to have you with us, even if it's only on a temporary basis. There are a few things I want to run by you while you're here, as well as working with you on the paper we've discussed. I know a mass of stuff's been done on the importance of clear lines of communication in a multi-disciplinary approach, but nothing definitive ever seems to come out of it.'

Prue turned in her chair and watched open-mouthed as her boss put out a hand and greeted the madman with every evidence of delight.

'You've met Prue. Famous. She'll be doing most of the hack work on the paper for me, so you'll be seeing a lot of each other.'

'Paper? What paper?' Prue demanded. Better to argue about that than the 'seeing a lot of each other' phrase which had prompted her dismay.

Mark grinned unrepentantly.

'I didn't tell you? What if the three of us get together after work? I'd ask Crystal to join us, but daren't risk Peter Barclay's wrath if I keep his pregnant wife after work. We can fill her in later. Five-thirty, my office. Catch you later, Will. You coming, Prue?'

Although used to Mark's briskly competent approach to work, Prue was still left feeling slightly breathless. She glanced across the table to see if 'Will' was similarly affected, and discovered his attention was once again on the files. No, not on the files, but on a scratch pad beside them, his whole being apparently focussed on the notes he was writing with a swift, bold hand.

She stood up, but the movement failed to divert him, so, thanking him politely for the coffee, she made her way to the door and was halfway out before Mark poked his head out of his office door.

'On second thoughts, stay there with Will,' he called to

her. 'You can introduce him to the children and parents, and watching any expert at work is instructive.'

Any expert at work?

Prue swung slowly back to where said expert was still totally focussed on whatever he was writing. How instructive could watching someone fill a page with black slanting writing be?

She was saved by Pat's arrival, and, feeling totally out of place, offered to get coffee for the therapy nurse.

'Thanks. Crystal's not far behind me. I saw her pulling into her parking space as I caught the lift. She'll have a cup of herbal tea; the bags are in that little green jar.'

Prue waited for Pat to acknowledge the other person in the room, or for him to nod a greeting to Pat, but no. Pat acted as if the six-foot pack of well-parcelled testosterone wasn't there, stripping off her light coat and hanging it on the hat stand in the far corner of the room, then tucking her handbag into the bottom drawer of the filing cabinet.

She must have sensed Prue's bewilderment, for she smiled and said, 'The Prof's worked with us before. It's absolutely useless talking to him when he's immersed in something else. You can say good morning like a civilised human being, even prattle on about the weather. He doesn't hear a word. Then later, when he finishes whatever he's doing, he greets you like a long-lost friend, and asks what the weather's like outside.'

Her smile became a chuckle.

'Makes you feel a right fool, it does. So now I wait until he surfaces, and do the polite thing then.'

Prue peered at the man Pat was discussing. He *must* be able to hear what was being said. But if he did, he gave no sign of it, although as she watched he completed whatever he was writing with one last bold flourish, then looked up to catch Prue watching him.

He looked puzzled for an instant, then smiled at her.

'A few thoughts occurred to me. For Mark's paper. If I don't write things down immediately, I find I can lose the intuitive spark that sometimes leads to the best answer.'

'How are you, Prof?'

Pat's voice made him turn, and Prue saw his smile broaden into a joyful grin.

'Pat! When did you sneak in? How's my favourite nurse?'

He stood up and enveloped Pat's stout frame in a bear-hug, but Prue wasn't taken in by this performance. The man *must* have seen and heard Pat come in. This was some act he put on. Pat called him 'Prof', no doubt because he played the absent-minded professor to attract attention.

The glasses certainly helped that academic image, but Prue wasn't fooled, not for one minute. In her experience, most men were into role-playing of some kind, whether to gain attention, win sympathy, fool women, or hide their true nature.

To cover a psychosis? Incipient madness?

Organise shoes for her, indeed!

She'd see about that.

Crystal bowled in at that stage, looking sickeningly healthy and radiantly beautiful. The seventh month of her pregnancy showed as a small neat bump, barely evident beneath the loosely flowing smock she wore over black leggings.

The hugging, kissing, and warm greeting routine was repeated, although Prue noticed Crystal called him William.

William!

The name suited him better than the diminutive Mark had used, Prue decided, eyeing the newcomer over the top of a file she was pretending to study.

'Is Ross Finch your first appointment?' Crystal asked him. 'He's outside with his mother. Pat, will you do the introductions and hang about as a familiar face?'

Pat, who'd been frowning over a long list she held in her hand, shook her head.

'Mark wants some old files pulled. He's got a clinic so Claire's busy—'

'He's left me here to do introductions,' Prue offered, although she was again puzzling over Mark's decision.

Were all locums offered the services of another staff member as back up on their first day? Or was she there as insurance?

Perhaps he *was* mad!

'Shall we go?'

She spun towards the source of her confusion, and caught a suggestion of a teasing warmth in the dark brown eyes. It was such a knowing look, so complicit, she wondered if reading minds was as easy for him as reading patient files.

Then he leaned towards her and touched her cheek, just as the alarm bells rang, signalling a code in some distant part of the hospital.

'You've a little piece of paper there,' he explained, flicking it away, but his dark eyes looked confused, as if the gesture—or perhaps the bells—had bothered him.

CHAPTER TWO

WILLIAM had heard those particular bells before, he reminded himself as he followed Prue towards the treatment room. They'd just startled him for an instant. Particularly as bending close to remove the little scrap of paper from the young doctor's skin had given him an opportunity to take another look at those pale freckles, and the bells had jarred him back to a realisation of where he was and what he was, supposedly, doing here.

The challenge of hands-on work in a clinic like this always excited William. The patients he saw as part of his teaching were different—the presence of students making those sessions more structured and formal.

'Rejuvenating!' he said to the woman he'd found sleeping on the table. 'That's the word.'

She cast a sidelong glance at him, and he grinned at the suspicion he could feel radiating from her.

'Coming in to these situations,' he explained. 'It reminds me what physio is all about. Renews my enthusiasm for the science at the most basic level.'

Her blue eyes widened slightly, disbelief still evident. He wondered more about the muscle control she'd need to achieve the effect than why she should be treating him with such reserve.

'Good morning, Ross. Mrs Finch.' His introducer nodded to the woman and squatted down in front of the child, who seemed small and thin for his age. 'This is—'

As she hesitated over his name, William joined her at near-floor level.

'William,' he said, and held out his hand to the little

boy. 'How do you do, Ross? I'm taking Annette's place for a while. Will you show me how you do your exercises?'

Dark curls bobbed as the boy nodded solemnly.

'Come on through,' William said. 'Dr Valentine has warmed the table for you this morning. Are you sore at the moment? Stiff?'

He glanced at Mrs Finch as he asked the questions and her smile told him more than the quick shake of her head.

'I've got a stiff knee, but it gets better when I run and play,' Ross admitted, leading his retinue into the treatment room with the confidence of a child quite at home in a hospital.

William's heart felt heavy, as it always did when he considered children suffering, but he knew being moved by what he saw and heard was an important part of his 'hands-on' policy. One of the reasons he took these locum jobs when he could spare the time.

He turned to Mrs Finch.

'How about you go first?' he suggested. 'Could you show me the exercises you and Ross do each day, and the order in which you tackle them? Just one of each, not full sets.'

He lifted the child to the table and stood back. Years of watching students had honed his powers of observation and he knew he'd spot any weaknesses in Mrs Finch's technique.

He could see the stiffness in the child's left knee and evidence of its resistance to straightening.

'Wonderful!' he said, when the woman had run through the routine and stepped back from the table.

He took her place, and spoke directly to the child.

'Do you know what we call the exercises Mummy does for you? The ones where she moves your foot or hand while you just lie there?'

Ross shook his head, his dark eyes fixed on William's face as he waited for an answer.

'They're called passive exercises. Passive means you're not doing much about it—like Dr Valentine here, and her exercise. Your mother's doing all the work, but what she's doing is still good for you because it's stretching the muscles and tendons to remind them what they're supposed to do all by themselves.'

He stepped up to the table, helped Ross into a sitting position with his legs stretched in front of him on the table.

'See how your left leg won't lie down flat. I'm going to add this exercise to your chart. I hold your leg here—' he took a gentle grip on the top of the calf muscle '—then with my other hand press down. Does that hurt?'

He watched Ross's face, knowing he was more likely to learn the truth from his expression than from his words. Some children suffered a false bravado which prevented them yelling when the pain grew bad, while others went the other way, and begged to stop at the first twinge. As he often told both students and the lecturers under him, judging tolerance levels was as important as judging how far to push treatment.

'Can you feel the stretch?'

Ross nodded.

'Very good! Excellent,' William told him. 'Did you feel the table under your knee? Sometimes, when you're sitting watching TV perhaps, you could do it yourself. Use your hands to press down on your knees, particularly that silly stiff one.'

He moved on to another exercise, again because he'd seen a weakness in the technique which he hoped he might be able to, tactfully, correct.

'Now you've got so good at ankle circles,' he said, lowering himself to the floor and stretching his own legs out in front of him, 'I want you to try something different.

Look, see how I make my circles. I'm keeping my legs still at the same time and just moving my feet. You try it, Dr Valentine. Show Ross how tricky it is.'

Limited floor space meant his Sleeping Beauty had to stretch out very close to him. Close enough for her to mutter, 'I don't do exercise, remember,' quite venomously in his ear.

He grinned at the response, but guessed she was playing along with him when she made a complete botch of the ankle circles.

'Hold your legs still,' William told her.

'Like this,' Ross piped up, and, as William had hoped, the child then demonstrated the correct way to do the exercise.

'Was that your not-so-subtle way of showing me how unfit I am?' Prue demanded, the moment the patient and his mother had departed and she must have felt released from her obligation to be polite.

'Of course not,' William replied. 'I did it to goad Ross into a top performance.'

She didn't look impressed. In fact, she looked downright suspicious.

'Are you looking for weaknesses in Annette's therapy technique? Is this some form of ongoing assessment?'

He was startled, then upset, and plunged into denial.

'Good heavens, no! She's an excellent therapist. I should know, I trained her myself.'

The final sentence had a smug sound to it, and he immediately wished he could retract it.

'You trained her yourself?'

Oh, for a system whereby one could erase the spoken word.

'Gross exaggeration, that,' he amended, 'but she was a student under me.' Unbridled student mirth echoed in his head! 'Er, well, not literally under me the way the jokesters make it sound. Never get involved with students. It was my motto from the start. I was young—some thought I was good-looking. Very dangerous, especially in this day and age. That's why I had Isobel, really. Made things so much easier to be engaged, but, yes, Annette studied under me.'

As his flow of words ceased, William looked at the woman who'd prompted them. Why on earth had he felt the need to expand on his original statement? And, having felt it, why stumble into such a morass of confusion?

The blueness of her eyes snagged his attention as she stared at him, then shook her head as if to clear it.

'I'm not going to attempt to unscramble that explanation,' she told him. 'But I gather Pat's calling you ''Prof'' isn't too wide of the mark. You're a professor?'

He smiled at the rank disbelief in her tone.

'Associate professor, actually. Professors of Physiotherapy are very thin on the ground worldwide.'

Again the blue eyes widened.

'It must be the orbital muscle of the orbicularis oculi that does it,' he muttered to himself, then realised he'd spoken aloud when his companion used a new set of muscles, her corrugator supercilii, to frown at him.

'I'm sorry. That sounded rude.' He tripped into the apology. 'I've been working on motor control of the deep muscles in the spine and joints and been sidetracked into a theory of retraining muscles that don't do much work to take over the work of ones that have become atrophied for some reason. I tend to think in muscle groups and, since you widened your eyes like that earlier, my subconscious must have started sorting out which muscle you were using to achieve the effect.'

'Oh, yes?'

The look she gave him reminded him of something else.

'The corrugator supercilii is the muscle that makes you frown. I tell my students it explains its own name—corrugates the skin with frown lines, super means above and cilium is the eyelash—but of course you'd know that. What fascinates me is that we get "supercilious" from the same source, don't we? An expression named for the muscle that produces it—well, more or less.'

Prue shook her head for about the fourth time in as many minutes.

'I can't believe this conversation,' she said. 'And I feel sorry for students who have to try to follow the convoluted workings of your brain. It's like watching a foreign movie with half the subtitles missing.'

He waited patiently for her to finish her complaint.

'That bad, huh?' he asked, appearing totally unabashed. 'Don't worry. It's the freedom from academic restraint. It goes to my head at first, but I'll settle down in a day or two. Who's next?'

He did his charming smile routine again and Prue had to steel herself against it.

'You've got the list,' she reminded him.

He passed it to her and pointed to the second name.

'Oh, Emma Ricco. She's suffering from Juvenile Rheumatoid Arthritis,' Prue explained. 'About twelve months ago, her parents opted for more aggressive steroid treatment in the hope that when the disease leaves her she'll have less permanent disability.'

'More aggressive treatment meaning the use of cortico-steroids instead of non-steroidal anti-inflammatory drugs?'

Prue nodded. He might waffle on, this man, and get off track, but he had a grasp on the wider picture as well.

'So, what's the effect of those as far as therapy's concerned?' He glanced at his watch, then cut her off before she could reply. 'No, we'll talk while the patient is with us. Better that way. It gets things across to the parent-caregiver as well without sounding as if we're delivering lectures.'

He flashed a brilliant version of 'the smile' at her and headed for the door. Prue used his tactic, trying to recall what muscle groups were employed in producing a smile, in the hope it would diminish the unwanted effect. Then, belatedly remembering she was supposed to be doing introductions, she hurried after him.

He was way past introductions. In fact, as Prue entered the waiting room he was on his knees in front of Emma, producing coins from her ear.

Mrs Ricco was gazing at the man with undisguised admiration.

He'd probably smiled at her, Prue decided.

'Ah, here's Dr Valentine. She's my off-sider today. Are we ready?'

He turned to Prue, and she managed to nod her agreement.

Ready for what? To sit on the floor and wiggle her ankles—unsuccessfully?

'—effects of corticosteroids?'

Prue dragged her mind away from recollections of the radiant heat of his body as they'd sat close together and tried to work out what he'd asked. It must be lack of sleep affecting her today, because radiant heat from colleagues' bodies had never bothered her before.

'Do you want the long list or just the reactions Emma has suffered?'

He was leading Emma into the treatment room, Mrs Ricco just behind him.

'Whatever springs to mind—not necessarily specific to Emma,' he said, and Prue closed her eyes, trying to visualise the page in her textbook where the possible side effects of prednisone, the corticosteroid of choice, were listed.

She mentioned the first that came to mind, ticking it off on her index finger.

'Increased appetite, though Mrs Ricco has been careful with Emma's diet, and you haven't turned into a butter-ball, have you, Emma?'

'No, and I don't eat chips or crisps any more,' Emma announced, prompting William to glance at Prue.

'Fluid retention?' he murmured.

Prue nodded, then listed off the other possible side effects.

'Increases also in sugar, fats and cholesterol in the blood. We arrange for Emma to have blood tests before every visit, to ensure these are kept at acceptable levels. But the worst side effect is the depression of the auto-immune system, leaving the child at risk of infection.'

'I can't ever go anywhere near anyone with chickenpox or I have to have an injection.'

Prue was startled by Emma's comment, and wondered, not for the first time, just how much of adult conversations children understood and retained.

'We've had to alert the school,' Mrs Ricco, who'd been running through Emma's exercise routine, explained. 'Ask them to let us know if there's any outbreak at all.'

William turned to Prue.

'Why chickenpox in particular?' he asked. 'Wouldn't Emma be at risk of any infectious disease?'

A man who knew what muscle made her eyes widen would naturally want to know every tiny detail of Emma's protocol, Prue realised.

'Yes, she's at risk of any infection. But in someone with a suppressed immune system, chickenpox can be exceedingly dangerous, attacking every organ in the body. Because of the severity of the disease in these cases, it's best to administer immunoglobulin within four days of contact with an infected person. Even a cough or a slight temperature is cause for concern, and Mrs Ricco has to monitor Emma's health fairly rigorously.'

Pleased she'd reached the end of the explanation without too much faltering, Prue relaxed, leaning forward to watch as William took over the exercises, gently moving Emma's limbs to assess the full range of movement.

'Any other side effects?' he asked, and Prue realised she hadn't finished after all.

'Rare ones. I've a list we give out to parents. I'll get you a copy later.'

He glanced at her and seemed about to argue, but must have sensed she'd stopped for some reason, and merely nodded his agreement.

As Prue watched him work, involving both the mother and the child, drawing out of Mrs Ricco the areas where she had difficulty, suggesting ways to cope, Prue acknowledged that Mark had been correct. It *was* good to watch an expert at work.

'You were happy to discuss some of the side effects in there,' he said, when they were back in the office for a break between patients and Prue had given him the list. 'Why the sudden reticence on the others?'

Prue eyed him warily. He'd gone directly to the bench by the rear wall and was fussing with the coffee-pot again, but possibly that was to mask his interest. Was he going to question everything she said and did? And, if so, just what would 'working with him' on a paper entail?

'You must have had a reason,' he prompted, turning his head to look at her, his dark eyes alert—as if eager for her reply.

'Emma's involved with the things I mentioned. She knows she must tell her mother if she feels sick. She's aware of what she should and shouldn't eat, and we've told her why, although, until today, I wasn't sure how much of it she understood.'

Prue paused, sorting the words she wanted to say into logical order. Not an easy task, given her lack of sleep.

Well, she supposed it was lack of sleep muddling her thought processes.

'Other side effects, like a temporary suppression of growth, could worry a child, and then the rarer side effects like osteoporosis, muscle weakness, increased blood pressure—that's always monitored—mood swings, thinning of the skin, stomach ulceration—you can see the number of them. Explaining them to a young patient could be counter-productive.'

'Particularly as not all of them will occur in every child? You'd have kids watching their skin to see if the blood's going to come pouring out?'

Prue had to smile at the image he conjured up, but she knew a child's mind could exaggerate the complication in precisely that way.

'Black, wasn't it?' he asked, and she realised he'd been fussing to some purpose. He turned towards her and set the beaker of coffee on the desk, a plate of biscuits beside it. 'Do you always see the child with a parent present? Or do you have some sessions with the one or other on their own?'

'Parents are usually present for therapy sessions and always for appointments with Mark. Once a child is comfortable in the unit, and knows the procedure, an aide will usually take him or her to Pathology, or Radiology, whatever's required, which gives Mark and the parent time to talk. Parents can make appointments to see Mark on their own, and can phone him any time. He makes a point of being accessible to them.'

William settled into the chair behind the desk and sipped at his coffee. He clasped long-fingered hands around his beaker as if to warm them, and leaned forward.

'And the current practice for passing information to the primary source of care—the child's GP? How does that work?'

'Does your mind always leap from bough to bough like an erratic chimpanzee?' Prue demanded. 'One minute we're talking about the side effects of corticosteroids and now we're onto lines of communication.'

'But that's why we're working together.'

William Alexander's wounded look was nearly as intriguing as his smile, Prue decided.

'I can't work with Mark to improve something if I don't know the system in place at the moment.' He checked his watch. 'No time now. Drink your coffee, have a biscuit, and we'll talk at lunch-time.'

Well, at least he's dropped the idea of running! Prue kept the thought to herself, not wanting to remind him of his earlier suggestion.

They worked through the morning, seeing three more patients, William questioning her about theoretical issues, discussing practical aspects of treatment with the children and their parents.

'Very impressive!' she told him as they finished with Jamie Blythe, and the excited little boy had left the room, clutching a new Star Wars figure William had produced from what must be a very capacious pocket. 'I know Annette has terrible trouble getting him to exercise. He's a manipulative little cuss and his parents are too soft-hearted for their own good. They fall for his ''not feeling well'' routine all the time. Getting him to pretend he was C3PO was a stroke of genius!'

A smile flirted around William's lips.

'I was wondering when something I did would meet with your approval,' he teased, and she felt her face grow hot.

'I've been impressed throughout,' she said stiffly. 'If I'd known you needed praise to boost your ego, I could have been uttering ''well dones'' at regular intervals throughout the morning.'

'Lack of sleep make you edgy, does it?' No smile, but

the crinkling at the corner of his eyes suggested he was still teasing her.

'I am not edgy,' she told him, but when he put his hand on the small of her back to steer her through the door in front of him, her body made a lie of the words, responding with a jerky movement that could probably be described as a skitter of alarm.

'No, not at all.'

The suave agreement made her want to kick him, but kicking physiotherapy locums was probably against hospital policy—as well as appearing extremely childish.

'You've a group therapy session this afternoon,' she told him, resolutely ignoring his taunts. 'Will you be able to manage that on your own? I'm due on duty upstairs at two.'

'Which gives us time for a walk in the park—prelude to the running—then a quick bite to eat. The shoes should be here by now.'

Again he touched her, only this time it was to ease her towards the therapists' office. And this time, she had the presence of mind not to leap into the air. Actually, she was too stunned by his pronouncement to move at all, and it was only pressure from his strong, warm hand that produced a forward motion.

'You didn't really order shoes for me, did you?' she stuttered, turning to look up into his face, then wishing she hadn't as she read the amusement in his eyes.

'Of course I did. I love a new project. You can be it for the month I'm here.'

'Mark has a project for you!' Prue protested. 'And I don't want to run—I don't want to be anyone's project.'

Somehow she'd got those sentences around the wrong way. Properly categorised, the not being anyone's project should have come first, not running second, and Mark's idea added as a sop for this bulldozer of a man.

'You only think you don't want to run,' he said, in a

kindly fashion, urging her into the office where the first thing she saw was a stack of shoe boxes.

'I don't believe this!' She closed her eyes, then cautiously opened them again. The boxes were still there.

'Humour me!' William Alexander asked. 'Just try on the shoes and find a pair that fits.'

'I do not want to run. Not today, not tomorrow, not any time.'

'You're saying you don't want to be fit?' he asked incredulously. 'I don't mean super-fit, athlete-level stuff, just fitter than you are? Healthier.'

'Well…' Prue began, unable to lie outright when at least once a day, usually after she'd panted up a flight of stairs instead of waiting for a lift, she made vows to begin some form of regular exercise.

He must have sensed a weakness, for he forged on.

'It won't cost you anything but a little sweat,' he said persuasively. 'I get the shoes for nothing. A couple of pairs a year because I recommend the shop to all my students. I haven't had the need to take up the offer this year until now. Come on, Prue, it will be fun, and we can talk and run at the same time.'

She shouldn't have looked at him, shouldn't have let the word 'fun' jolt her into the realisation that it had been a long time since she'd done anything 'just for fun'!

'I can barely breathe and run at the same time, let alone talk!' she told him, and knew, as soon as his smile lit up his face, that he'd taken her acerbic response as agreement.

'Sit!' he ordered. 'I'll fit them for you. Did they send socks? Ah, yes! And there's the track suit!'

My head will fall off if I keep shaking it at his antics, Prue decided, but, in her tired state, obeying was easier than arguing. She sat, slipped her feet out of her shoes, and waited, vaguely discomfited when he knelt in front of her.

'Are these stockings, or one of those all in one garments

women wear these days?' he asked, but as he'd touched her ankle at the same time it took a moment for her to grasp the meaning of his question.

'Why?' she demanded, shifting her suddenly susceptible ankle out of reach of his fingers.

He glanced up at her, his face impassive.

'Well, stockings you could probably detach and slip off quite easily, while taking off tights—is that the right word?—might be trickier. I'll turn around if you feel embarrassed.'

Useless to tell him she was beyond feeling anything but constant and varying levels of astonishment in his presence.

Although—

Perhaps he was teasing her! Pushing her to get a reaction. The bland look on his face hid any hint of what he might be thinking.

Two could play at that game, she decided, and she stood up, so close to him she could see the neat part in his hair and paleness of his scalp, contrasting to the dark reddish brown, along the line.

'If I need to take off my stockings to embark on this ridiculous programme, why didn't you say so?' she said, and hitched up her skirt to find the suspenders on the left, unhooked them front and back, and slid down that stocking.

He knelt motionless at her feet, but she knew he'd seen the extra bit of leg she'd deliberately revealed, though he was careful not to react to her behaviour.

She took the next one off more slowly, not because she wanted him to see more, but because the clasp was stiff, or stuck, or her fingers had suddenly become clumsy. He began to hum, and when she worked out it was 'The Stripper', she chuckled.

'Okay!' she said. 'Let's call it quits.'

He grinned up at her, and she felt a surge of warmth—not the embarrassed kind this time, but the warmth that came from finding someone who might turn out to be a friend.

'I didn't for a minute believe you *would* wear stockings,' he admitted. 'I thought all women went for the easy option these days.'

'Not when they can be wearing the same clothes for twenty-four hours, they don't. Well, not this woman, anyway.'

She slid her stockings off her feet and tossed them under the chair, then took the socks he offered her and pulled them on.

Maybe it *will* be fun, she told herself, watching as William's slim fingers threaded laces through eyelets, his head bent as if even this mechanical task demanded total concentration.

Then he took hold of her right foot, and she felt her nerve endings respond so swiftly it was all she could do not to pull away.

Talk about inappropriate reactions! she chided herself. A man touches your ankle and you go into heated confusion. What are you? Miss Victoriana? Think of him as a shop assistant. You don't break out in goose-bumps when they touch your feet.

She continued to lecture herself as he tied the laces, then put on the second shoe for her and laced it up.

'Stand up!' he told her and she obeyed.

'Now walk around. How do they feel? Where are they tight? What do you think?'

'They're fine,' she told him, although they were more than fine. They made her feel as if she were walking on a cloud, made her want to bounce up and down a little, maybe even jog!

The man's mesmerised you, she told herself.

'Just fine,' she repeated, hoping sounding sensible would make her feel more that way.

'Perhaps you should try another pair,' he suggested.

And have you kneeling in front of me, touching my feet, upsetting my nerves?

'No way. If I find another pair that feels as good I'd have to make a decision—which is not my forte where clothes are concerned. These fit, they don't pinch anywhere, I'll take them, but I don't for a minute believe in the benevolence of a sports shop that gives you two free pairs of shoes a year. Pass me the box so I can check the price. I'll pay you for them.'

He passed the box without argument, and only when she looked at it and realised it didn't have a price tag on it did she realise why he'd obeyed.

'Very clever!' she told him. 'But it shouldn't be too hard for me to find out how much they were.'

'Do you always argue?' he asked. 'About everything? Or only exercise and money?

His eyes smiled at her as he asked the questions, and she had no idea what muscles he was using to achieve *that* effect. All she felt was its power to mesmerise her.

'Shouldn't we be on our way?' She changed the subject to avoid answering an unanswerable question. Maybe running was a good idea—running as far and as fast as she could. The man was no spring chicken. He was probably married with half a dozen children. Hadn't he mentioned someone called Isobel?

'You'd be more comfortable in the track suit,' he suggested, passing her trousers and a zip-fronted jacket in a vivid electric blue. 'They've put in this as well,' he added, pulling a T-shirt from the plastic bag. 'And this!'

'And this' was a leotard with a pattern of navy in the same electric blue as the track suit. It seemed incredibly skimpy in spite of the fact it had legs in it.

'I'll take the T-shirt,' Prue told him, 'to wear under the

track-suit top. I think I'd put the park regulars off their lunch if I appeared in a leotard.'

She felt his gaze skim her body.

'I doubt that,' he said mildly, but he handed her the more concealing garments and dismissed her with a nod.

If she took a really long time getting changed, then maybe...

CHAPTER THREE

PRUE emerged from the washroom feeling so conspicuous she had to fight an urge to slink along the walls. Not that slinking helped.

'Wow!' Kerry Byrne, one of the outpatient nurses, commented, while a porter whistled loudly.

'Surely it would be more sensible to make clothes like this in black or navy,' she grumbled at William as she returned to the therapists' office.

'But that colour suits you. Makes your eyes bluer. I guessed as much and specifically asked for blue. Brown wouldn't do a thing for you and I imagine anything green would make you look sallow.'

'Gee, thanks a heap!' Prue muttered at him. 'Any more compliments?'

He'd changed into a track suit in a faded brown velour-like material and looked—

Even sexier than he had earlier in his glasses?

Married with children, she reminded herself.

A ship passing in the night.

Here this month and gone next.

You don't need a man in your life.

None of these mental exhortations reduced his appeal one iota, but at least they kept her from arguing as he led the way out through the Outpatient entrance.

'We'll take it slowly, no running at all for the first day, warming up with a gentle walk. Followed by some brisk walking to get your heart rate up, then a cooling-off stroll back. Okay?'

He turned the beaming smile on her again and she nodded weakly, then had to hurry as his 'walking slowly' pace took him several strides ahead of her immediately.

'This is slowly?' she demanded as she caught up.

'Very slowly,' he assured her. 'So, tell me how you keep in touch with the patients' local doctors.'

Prue hoped her legs would keep moving without direct orders, because she'd need all her mental agility to answer the questions he would, no doubt, be firing at her.

'As far as Mark is concerned, he sends a letter to the child's GP, or the group practice where the child is registered, after each visit. If he's had occasion to speak to another member of the team, the dietitian, ophthalmologist, orthopaedic surgeon, therapist et cetera, he adds information from them, but that's only if something has changed in either the child's treatment or status.'

'So therapists don't issue a separate report?'

'Not every visit.'

They were walking towards the lake and Prue took in the sight of massed daffodils, brought into bloom by the unseasonably warm late March weather. They spread in such bright beauty across the grass, she was glad she'd been bullied into coming outside. Although she guessed William might just as well be exercising in the dark for all the notice he was taking of his surroundings.

'And what about vice versa?' he asked, confirming her guess that he was totally focussed on his questions. 'As primary caregiver, what's the regular doctor's role?'

'He looks after all the normal things—well-child visits, inoculations, minor ailments. He also arranges a lot of the regular blood tests and has the results copied to us at the unit so, when a child comes in, Mark has all the information he needs at his fingertips.'

'But you still do blood tests here.' William reminded her of her words earlier in the day.

'In certain circumstances,' Prue agreed.

He'd upped the pace and she began to feel the unaccustomed exercise heating her thighs, making them itchy, but, as yet, no muscles were protesting.

'Computer links would be the answer,' William said.

'Some GPs are already linked to the pathology services, and a few who have patients with us are linked through to the unit. We're getting there,' she told him.

'Perhaps a form,' he mused. 'Something that could be easily adapted for computer use eventually but in the meantime will cut down on duplication of effort, not to mention paper usage. Ticks for no change, columns for changes to be written, a space for comments. I wonder…'

Prue left him wondering, taking advantage of his ruminations to breathe in the fresh, still crisp air, and silently admit to a sense of well-being as the green of the grass, the fragile early blossom on the trees and the brilliant colour of the sun-kissed daffodils filled an empty place in her soul.

'Now we about-turn, walk briskly for a very short while, then dawdle. Always walk the horse slowly back to the stable to allow him to cool down—that's a good rule for humans as well.'

Brought rudely out of her reverie about sunshine and daffodils, Prue was too busy keeping up with his 'briskly' to object to the horse analogy. She trotted alongside him, gasping for air, protesting with what little breath she had.

'You said no running today, but how can I not run when you get those ridiculously long legs into motion?'

He turned and grinned at her.

'I thought it was too good to last,' he teased.

'What was?' she demanded, huffing out the words with difficulty.

'You not arguing,' he elaborated. 'Far too good to be true.'

He slowed down—not, she suspected, because she was

having trouble keeping up, but to do with the horse cooling off.

'As it happens I was admiring the beauty of the park,' she told him huffily. 'Something you probably failed to notice.'

His eyes twinkled with delight.

'Daffodils and pink blossoms got to you, did they?' he said. 'Touched your soul with their beauty?'

She was about to protest at his derision, even though his words echoed her thoughts almost exactly, when he added, 'It never fails to get to me, either. People rave on about the glorious Mediterranean coastline, or the stark beauty of the Arizona desert, but give me an English park in spring and a field of golden daffodils, and I go to mush inside.'

Prue peered suspiciously at him, certain he was having her on, but his face was serious, his lips lifted in a small smile, as if going to mush inside was of great satisfaction to him.

A complex man, this William Alexander!

For a start, how likely was it that a professor—correction, associate professor—would make a habit of doing hands-on locums? Professors of any persuasion were academics, their career paths plotted early, a leaning towards scholarship and teaching keeping them away from real people, safe from the world's intrusion, in their ivory towers.

So he was doing a paper with Mark—but surely that didn't necessitate working in the unit?

'Do you lunch in the canteen?' His question startled her, and she realised they'd negotiated the road crossing while she pondered the enigma of William Alexander, and were now approaching the front entrance to the hospital. 'Could I join you, seeing as I don't know anyone here?'

'Don't know anyone?' Prue echoed. 'That kite won't fly! What about Pat and Crystal? And the bouncy nurse in

Outpatients who greeted you like a long-lost lover as we were heading out on this walk?'

'We could talk about communication so we've some ideas to put to Mark this afternoon,' he continued, deftly ignoring her protests.

'Communication is a two-way street,' Prue reminded him bitterly. 'One person talks and the other listens!'

But she knew she'd end up eating lunch with him. Saying no to him was as futile as trying to stop a bulldozer with—

A bunch of daffodils?

'I need to shower and change,' she told him. 'And I'm back on duty at two.'

He nodded absent-mindedly and she guessed his attention had already shifted to something else, her acquiescence taken for granted.

Not that things worked out that way. She was bleeped before she reached the mess, needed on the ward as a child with unexplained swelling of his knee was coming up from A and E.

'He was seen by an orthopaedic registrar down there, but, as his history shows he had a swollen ankle a couple of weeks ago, the registrar consulted Dr Gregory and they're admitting him for tests.'

Holly Harvey, on duty in the medical ward, explained this to Prue over the phone, adding that it might be best if she was there when the child arrived so she could clerk him.

Forgoing the shower, she headed for the ward.

'His name's Michael. He's only a baby. Why does the doctor want him to stay? Why not give him some medicine to make the swelling go down and send him home?'

Prue guessed the tense and frightened woman asking these questions at the nurses' station was her patient's mother. The small child who clung, limpet-like, to the woman's chest, would be her new patient.

She raised her eyebrows towards Holly and received a confirmatory nod.

'I'm Prue Valentine, I work with Dr Gregory,' she said gently to the distraught parent. 'Let's go over to Michael's bed and talk there.'

She put her arm around the woman's shoulders and helped support her as they followed Holly to the bed that had been prepared for Michael. Prue eased her into a chair that was drawn up close to the bed.

Holly produced a fluffy monkey, a bright plastic ball, and a small yellow duck from the locker beside the bed. She lined the toys up on the bed.

'You can play with these while Dr Prue talks to Mummy,' she told Michael, then she gave the mobile of garishly painted birds that hung above the bed a quick flick to get it moving. 'Or watch the pretty birds.'

Michael buried his head in his mother's shoulder, but as soon as Holly left the cubicle he lifted it to look at the birds, then reached out tentatively for the monkey, stroking the fur with his forefinger.

'I didn't bring any of his own toys. I never for a minute expected to have to stay!' his mother said.

'We'll work out some way to get his favourite toys to him, Mrs Leski,' Prue assured her, glancing at the file Holly had handed her to find the woman's name. 'And clothes for you and him—if you decide to sleep over.'

'How can I stay, with my other kids to think about? Who'll take care of them, collect them from school? He can't stay in hospital!'

She began to cry, and Michael, probably distressed by his mother's emotion, joined in, wailing lustily.

It gave Prue time to read what Mark had written. He wanted a bone-marrow test, and with such a young child—

Michael had just celebrated his first birthday—the marrow would be removed under a light general anaesthetic.

She waited patiently for Mrs Leski's sobs to subside, handed the woman some tissues from a box on the locker, and picked up the monkey to distract Michael while his mother composed herself.

'We'll sort out something for your other children,' she promised the woman. 'If necessary the hospital can arrange a carer through the community health service in your area, but right now let's talk about Michael and the tests he has to have. The sooner we get on to them, the sooner we can send you both home.'

The woman sniffed but nodded.

'Our own doctor fixed up for Michael to have a blood test last week and he didn't have to go to hospital for that. And my husband had blood tests when he was sick last year but he didn't have to go to hospital to have them,' she said. 'And my aunt's got arthritis, and that's what the doctor thought Michael had, but my aunt doesn't go to hospital for it.'

'There are no particular tests for juvenile arthritis,' Prue broke in before other relatives' ailments could be brought into the conversation. 'It's mainly a matter of ruling out other diseases.'

'Like what?'

Prue hesitated. Leukaemia in children could begin with leg pain, and, in a child younger than the usual onset for JRA, it would have to be ruled out with a conclusive bone marrow test before other diagnoses were considered. Particularly when a blood test showed anaemia. She'd seen that mentioned on Michael's recent test results, apparently relayed on through his GP to Mark, who'd made a note and circled it.

Should she explain this and upset Mrs Leski even more? And have her worrying over something that might not be?

The fact that Mark had been called to see Michael meant the physician who first saw the child at the hospital considered some form of arthritis the most likely cause of the swelling.

'Infection,' she said, reading ahead while she considered options, and noticing Mark had also ordered arthrocentesis. 'The specialist will take some fluid from Michael's knee. If the swelling is caused by an infection, it will show up and we can treat it with antibiotics. If it is an infection, the sooner it's treated, the better.'

'What else do they look for?' Mrs Leski asked as Michael relaxed enough to turn his attention to the duck.

'We'll do a general screening of Michael's blood, liver-function tests, kidney-function tests, check his urine. This will provide us with a base for him, so once he starts on medication, if Dr Gregory is confident it's arthritis, we can judge how the medication is affecting him.'

She paused, as always wanting to tell parents what to expect, but wondering at the same time where the explanations tipped over into information overload.

'Arthritis is a disease that stems from the immune system. Bone marrow creates antibodies that fight infection in the body, but sometimes the production goes haywire and some bodies start producing autoantibodies which fight good cells.'

'That sounds like what happens in cancer,' Mrs Leski said, and her arms tightened around Michael.

'It is similar, but in arthritis, these autoantibodies attack cells in joints, causing inflammation and pain. There are a couple of these autoantibodies that sometimes, not always, show up in blood tests of patients with juvenile rheumatoid arthritis. One's called rheumatoid factor or RF and the others are antinuclear antibodies or ANAs.'

Mrs Leski shook her head.

'So why can't they just test his blood for these RFs and ANAs and tell us he's got it or he hasn't?'

'Because they don't always show up in the blood, and in some cases a child can have ANAs in his or her blood and not have arthritis. I know it's very confusing, but please believe me when I say that, the more we can find out about Michael's health now, the better we can treat him in the future.'

'I suppose you have to do what you have to do,' Mrs Leski said. 'I'd better phone my husband. He's been on a special course up north but he's driving back today. I can get him on the cell phone, and he'll organise something for the kids. They might be right nuisances at times, men, but it's good to have them to fall back on when you need them. Not that he'll do much. He'll phone either my mum or his mum and sweet-talk one of them into taking over.'

Prue smiled at the wry admission.

'I'll bring a phone to you here. Now, what about a cup of tea and a sandwich?'

'That would be lovely. And Michael's probably hungry, although he's been off his tucker lately.'

'I'll check with Dr Gregory and find out what he's got scheduled. If he's managed to make time for the bone-marrow extraction this afternoon, he won't want Michael eating or drinking until after it.'

She slipped away, asking an aide to organise a snack for Mrs Leski, a young nurse to plug in a phone for the anxious mother, then she rang Mark from the nurses' station to check on his timetable.

'So I can send him to X-ray as soon as I've clerked him, then up to theatre at four-thirty?' she confirmed when he'd explained his projected timetable. 'Who's doing the anaesthetic? Well, whoever you get, can you ask him or her to hold off the preliminary visit until as late as possible? And what about the meeting for five-thirty? That still on?'

She listened to Mark run through his afternoon schedule and explain that he'd do the arthrocentesis at the same time. In reply to an anxious query, she assured him she'd entertain the physio locum if Mark was running late.

'With a song and dance routine, no doubt,' she muttered to herself as she returned to Michael's cubicle.

Mrs Leski was talking on the phone, so Prue mimed what she was about to do, and, keeping Michael distracted with the duck, she slipped a pressure cuff on his arm and inflated it, watching the mercury rise then fall, noting down the results.

She took an axillary measurement of his temperature. With no suspicion of fever, she didn't want to upset him with any procedures he could find threatening.

The phone call finished as the tray with tea and sandwiches arrived. Prue felt her stomach gurgle—the sticky bun seemed a long time ago—but, while Michael's mother had the distraction of her snack, it was best to take down both the child's and the relevant bits of the family's history.

'Call me Maureen,' Mrs Leski began in answer to Prue's first question. 'He's always loved getting up in the morning. Before it was light, he'd be on his feet, rattling the walls of his cot, wanting to be set free. Usually Peter, who's seven and sleeps in the same room, would lift him out and they'd have a little play. But, lately, Michael hasn't been pulling himself up and when Peter's tried to lift him out, he's cried.'

Maureen looked embarrassed.

'I yelled at Peter a few times, because I thought he must have bumped Michael. Poor Peter. He's the gentlest of all my children, and he adores the baby.'

Prue asked the obvious question, and Maureen listed off the names and ages of Michael's six older siblings.

'Seven kids! That's a handful,' she said, writing furiously to keep up with the flow.

Maureen smiled.

'I love each and every one of them—there's not one I'd be without. We decided very early on to have a whole tribe of kids, but, with the cost of everything going up all the time, we knew Michael had better be the last. Now this has happened!'

Fearing another bout of tears, Prue hurried into questions about whether Michael had shown any other symptoms apart from what could possibly have been morning stiffness and pain.

'Any fever, rash, loss of interest in playing games, changes in his normal behaviour?'

'He hasn't been sick, if that's what you mean, but he was nearly walking, going around and around all the furniture, or walking with the older kids holding his hands, even taking one or two steps on his own, but recently he hasn't done that. Just sits and plays.'

'When did you first notice this?' Prue asked, then immediately wished she'd phrased it better. She didn't want Maureen feeling guilty about not doing something earlier. 'Not that it's easy to pinpoint something like that,' she added, hoping that would soften the demand.

'I guess it could be a couple of weeks ago. He fell over the cat one day, and cried for a while, then after that the other kids would tease him to try to walk. They used to fight to help him, and were all so keen for him to start.'

She wiped away a stray tear.

'My husband's a nurse and he usually checks the kids' health, but, as I said, he's been away, so I took Michael to the doctor—after the cat accident—but he did a blood test and apart from being a bit anaemic which Susie is as well— she gets run-down easily and we thought he might be like her—there wasn't anything he could find. I told the kids to stop bothering him. I know kids reach these levelling-off stages in their development—they go so far then stop for a while. Gives them time to grow, my mother always says. Anyway, that's about how long ago it was.'

'Was his knee swollen at the time?'

Maureen thought for a moment, then shook her head.

'It mustn't have been because I thought he'd hurt his ankle. I can't recall if it was swollen, but I do know I thought it was the ankle bothering him.'

'And members of your family, have any of them any arthritic complaints, back problems, psoriasis—?'

'But psoriasis is a skin disease,' Maureen interrupted. 'My mum gets it. Like a rash on her elbows and her upper arms.'

'It's associated with arthritis and often comes together with arthritic pain in the fingers or toes.'

'I'll ask her about pain in her fingers,' Maureen said, 'but she's never mentioned it to me.'

Prue moved on down her mental list.

Recent travel or contact with anyone with an infectious disease, any previous illness, sibling illnesses or infections, and on until the sketchy admission notes had been expanded into an encapsulated history of the child and his immediate family.

She checked on the list of tests Mark wanted run, detached the sheet for the pathology lab, the note for X-ray, and excused herself to find out if someone was available to walk Maureen and Michael through the next stage of their hospital visit.

'I'll phone ahead to X-ray and explain about the scan,' she told the nurse who'd volunteered to go along. 'Just try to keep things moving. He's scheduled for theatre at four-thirty and you know how touchy they can get about late arrivals.'

She returned to Michael's bed and introduced the nurse, explained again what would happen next, then saw them out of the ward.

'I know I caught you before you were ready to come on duty, and, from the look of you, you want a shower, but Penny Wright's vein's collapsed. Could you try to insert another cannula?' Holly asked as soon as Prue was free. 'I thought we had her this time. She's been right since you got it into her foot during the night. Should we consider an intraosseus?'

Prue thought about it. Penny was a frail child with un-diagnosed but multiple disabilities. She had been born with poor muscle tone, and it was a miracle—or a tribute to her parents' faith, love and persistence—that had kept her alive for three years. Now, with a severe lung infection and no reserves of stamina with which to fight it, she was literally being kept alive by the intravenous fluid running into her.

'I don't think we should put her through the pain of an intraosseous but I'll speak to Caroline and Justin. See what they say.'

Prue checked the tray Holly had prepared with a new over-the-needle catheter, commercial heat pad to warm and dilate the vein, a syringe filled with saline to flush out the T-connector, adhesive tape, gauze, gloves—everything she'd need.

A curtain was drawn around Penny's bed, and Prue set the tray down outside, wanting to speak to the parents be-fore appearing with all the paraphernalia as if their assent were nothing but a formality.

As she eased the curtain apart the murmur of voices stopped, so she wasn't surprised to see Caroline and Justin both turned towards her as she entered.

What did surprise her—actually who—was William Alexander, sitting beside Penny's bed, the slight, limp form of the little girl held gently against his broad chest.

'Haven't you got a group therapy session?' she de-manded, speaking far more abruptly than she'd intended as shock shook her brain cells into disorder.

'In another five minutes,' the man said calmly, not even bothering to glance at his watch to confirm his placid statement.

Prue hesitated. It was really none of her business where he was, or what he was doing.

Caroline rescued her.

'William's an old friend. We'd lost touch lately, but Justin bumped into him this morning—they were both buying sticky buns—and he popped up to see us.'

'Holly tells me another vein's collapsed,' Prue said, deciding the best thing she could do was ignore the man who had erupted so forcibly into her life only hours earlier. 'I can try to find another one, or you could consider—'

Justin held up his hand for her to stop, then took Caroline's hand. He opened his mouth as if to speak, then closed it again and looked across at William.

'They would like to take Penny home.' William spoke as if he'd rehearsed the words. He rubbed the tip of his forefinger down the child's cheek as he spoke. 'Being up here all day and all night is taking its toll of both of them. I've said I can arrange a private nurse to sit with her at night. That way they can get some sleep in their own beds and be more alert to talk and sing to her during the day.'

'What about the IV—the fluids? I know the antibiotics aren't making any headway with the infection, but they're holding it. With some fiddling with a private nurse's schedule, could we—?'

She found herself addressing William, and, realising the mistake, turned towards the couple. Tears were sliding down Caroline's cheeks, their counterparts glistening in Justin's eyes.

'We don't want her to have to suffer any longer. No more drugs, no more drips, no more needles and veins collapsing,' Justin explained. 'We've talked about it and we'd rather take her home to her own room, to her familiar surroundings, and look after her there until the end comes.'

Prue blinked away her own emotion.

'Have you spoken to Jeremy Kerr about it?' she asked, knowing he was the consultant in charge of Penny's care.

'I phoned him, and he'll go along with it,' William told her.

Go along with it? The phrase seemed out of character for Jeremy, almost casual.

'They weren't his exact words,' William added, and his uncanny percipience made Prue shiver.

'Do you want an ambulance transfer?' she asked Justin, but again it was William who replied.

'I'll drive them all home as soon as I finish my session,' he said. 'Could you explain to Mark that I won't be able to make it at five-thirty? Maybe we could do a breakfast meeting instead. Give me your home phone number and I'll call you after I've set things up with him.'

And once again Prue found herself obeying, meekly reciting off her phone number when she should be telling him a breakfast meeting wouldn't suit her. It was her day off, for one thing.

She had missed nights' sleep to catch up on.

Lunch was the earliest meal she'd consider having—maybe even dinner.

She'd tell him so tonight.

Caroline stood up and crossed the room to kiss her on the cheek.

'Thank you for everything you've done,' she said. 'No one was as gentle with our Penny as you were.'

Now Prue had to blink hard to clear the sudden smeariness from her eyes, and to gulp down the stupid lump that formed in her throat.

CHAPTER FOUR

WILLIAM phoned at seven—not so absent-minded after all.

'It's William,' he said. 'William Alexander.'

As if she might know forty-seven Williams!

'Have you eaten?'

Still working on his introductory style, Prue was blustered into the truth.

'No,' she told him. 'I've barely had time to strip off that track suit and take a bath, let alone thinking about eating.'

'You wore your track suit home?'

'You say that as if wearing the wretched thing home was akin to parading down Regent Street in a G-string!' she retorted. 'I was bleeped before I had time to shower after our exercise. I was late off duty. Climbing into my car and driving home in the track suit seemed a reasonable option to me!'

'Well, don't forget to take it to work with you in the morning,' he warned. 'I can't get an unlimited supply, you know.'

She wasn't sure which point to make first—the fact that tomorrow was her day off and the only exercise she intended having was to turn over occasionally in her bed.

Or there was the argument about who was paying for her new, unwanted clothes...

Then there was the fact that, if they were hers, it was none of his business where she kept them.

'The address!' he said, in a voice that suggested long-suffering patience. Was he repeating the words? What had he asked? 'I can't collect you to take you out to eat if I don't know where you live.'

The explanation caused further confusion.

'I didn't say I'd go out and eat with you,' Prue protested, then rather spoilt things by adding, 'Did I?'

'Not exactly, but as you haven't eaten and I haven't eaten and from your phone number you're close by, it will give us a chance to talk before we see Mark.'

'You used that excuse to make me exercise at lunch-time,' Prue reminded him.

'Then what if I tell you I need company?' he said, throwing her totally off balance. Especially when she remembered little Penny, and guessed why the man didn't want to be alone right now.

'You must have dozens of friends who'd keep you company.'

And possibly a wife, she added to herself.

'A quick bite, that's all,' William tempted. 'Save you cooking. I'll pay.'

It was about here in the conversation that William began to realise it wasn't going too well. He hadn't analysed why it was important for him to see Prue Valentine tonight, but as he'd left Caroline and Justin's house he'd had an urge to talk to her.

Probably because she knew Penny, knew what was happening—and what would be likely to happen tonight or tomorrow.

'Please?'

He hoped he didn't sound too plaintive. Isobel had some-times objected to what she called a 'take pity on me' approach, although *he* invariably fell for it when women used it.

'That was a pathetic "please", William Alexander,' the particular woman he wanted to see said bluntly. 'A con job if ever I heard one. But you're right. I have to eat, and my own company isn't particularly enlivening tonight.'

There was a pause, then she gave him an address, only a couple of blocks away in South Kensington.

'I'll meet you downstairs in fifteen minutes; the buzzer doesn't always work,' she added, then he heard a click as she hung up.

An image of her eyes, as blue as the sky had been against the blossom in the park, flickered on the screen of his mind.

'This is business,' he reminded himself, quelling another memory of Isobel—this time her accusation that he was a closet romantic.

'You want bells and lights and whistles when you kiss the one you truly love. You want the whole deal, the hearts and flowers, a rainbow, and probably bluebirds. What we had was comfortable for you, like a safety net, but you're never going to find the love you truly need while you're hiding behind my skirts.'

And with that, she'd cut him adrift, taken away his security blanket, and left him lonely for companionship, celibate, and, eventually, relieved.

Not that he was going to admit that to her or anyone else.

And she was wrong about the bells and lights and whistles.

She had to be!

He blanked the image of 'drown-in' blue eyes from his mind and tackled a mental exercise, the drawing-up of a simple form that could be used for regular updates of information to GPs and practices.

Which was why he was meeting Prue Valentine.

Prue opened the front door to find him there, his hand lifted as if he was about to try the door handle. He was wearing pale bone-coloured trousers, and a chocolate-brown shirt that matched his eyes almost exactly.

'Your jacket matches your eyes almost exactly,' he said,

confusing her from that first instant by saying her thoughts aloud.

'I like blue,' she said abruptly. What else could she say once she ruled out, 'Don't do that to me!', which would have sounded peculiar, to say the least?

He studied her for a moment longer, then nodded as if satisfied by whatever had been going on inside his head.

'Do you like Turkish food? Have you tried Mustafa's?'

'Yes and yes,' she told him, feeling more comfortable with the practical turn in the conversation. 'It's a good choice at this time of the evening as most of the regulars there seem to eat later.'

She was congratulating herself on how well she was handling things, when he took her hand and tucked it into the crook of his elbow.

'Doesn't your arm get tired, holding it bent like that?' she asked, more to hide her own reaction to this simple politeness than out of interest in his well-being.

'I've never noticed it getting tired,' he replied, then he glanced her way and smiled. 'But, then, I'm fit!'

She saw the little crinkle of lines at the corner of his eyes, and wondered how old he might be.

Not that it mattered.

'My parents were well into their forties when I arrived as a surprise package,' he continued. 'As a result, my manners seem dreadfully dated to some people, but if I'm walking with a woman I like to feel I'm close enough to her to be of some use if she happened to need protection.'

'Murder and mayhem on the streets of South Ken,' Prue joked, which was easier than admitting there was something nice in the gesture—a certain allure in feeling protected.

And the radiant heat thing was working again.

'Inside or out?' he asked, and Prue awoke from her consideration of body heat and glanced around. The evening was fine enough for tables to have been set up outside, their privacy ensured by a concealing row of potted plants.

'Outside would be lovely. Who knows when we'll have another chance?'

'To eat together? We could do it often, if you liked.' He seemed surprised but did the polite thing very well for someone who'd taken her casual remark the wrong way.

'I meant because of the weather,' Prue told him. 'I mean it's only March and we're having fine weather. How many more evenings will we not have rain?'

'Oh, the weather?' William muttered, but he was looking at her with a puzzled frown on his face.

She would have asked him what was wrong, but an ambulance was weaving through the traffic on the road and, with its flashing lights and whooping siren, conversation was impossible.

'Definitely not bells,' she thought she heard him mutter, but as the phrase made no sense at all she dismissed it from her mind, and followed the young waitress to a table tucked up against the front of the restaurant.

While she studied the menu, he talked about Turkey, which he'd apparently visited frequently.

'Why Turkey?' she asked, when she'd given her order of *barbunya*, a bean dip, to begin and *küzü şiş*, the marinated lamb shish kebabs, to the hovering waitress.

William ordered the same things, but whether because he actually shared her taste in Turkish food, or from some form of politeness, Prue couldn't guess.

'I like the heat and the sunshine and the people,' he said, in answer to her query. 'So enthusiastic in everything they do—whether it's talking, or eating, or drinking.'

'A contrast to the ''show no emotion'' of the Brits?' she teased, and he responded with a smile that made her knees tingle.

'My father was very much that way,' he admitted. 'Although I hate categorisations and generalisations about different races.'

'You've done it yourself with your Turks,' Prue reminded him, and again he flashed the smile, only this time it made her head spin.

Lack of food, that's all it was, she told herself, and directed the conversation to a subject where smiles might be less likely.

'Well, what's your big idea about communication? Isn't that why we're here?'

He seemed confused, but only for instant, soon launching into a complicated explanation about spreadsheets adapted to paper use but easily computerised where or when possible.

Prue's ears buzzed and her eyelids grew heavy. She pasted what she hoped was an intelligent look on her face and gave up trying to follow his explanations. She'd have more hope of staying awake if she did something positive—like watching the way his lips moved as he spoke, or how the light from a street lamp fell across his face, the contrasting shadows accentuating strongly defined cheek bones and the hollow plains beneath them.

'You're falling asleep again.'

The pained reproach made her smile.

'You must admit the use of spreadsheets in electronic communication isn't the most riveting conversation for someone who's been up for thirty-six hours.'

'But you started it,' he complained. 'I was quite happy talking about travel and national personalities, about anything but work, in fact.'

She was startled by this admission, and was about to ask why, in that case, he'd asked her out, when she remembered Penny.

He'd wanted company.

And she'd fallen asleep!

'What made you choose physio?' she asked, relying on the tried and true social ploy of asking questions about one's companion.

He studied her for a moment—and then a little longer. His gaze moved across her face with an intensity that sent her nerves onto full alert.

'Trying to decide if I'm the right person to be trusted with your reasoning?' she said, attempting to lighten the suddenly electrified atmosphere between them.

He grinned and the tension snapped, leaving a companionable feeling in its wake.

'Trying to decide if you're being polite or really interested,' he retorted.

'Would it matter? Make a difference to your reply?'

Prue tried a smile of her own as she tossed the ball back into his court.

'Probably not,' he admitted. 'I'd always imagined myself in an academic life—my parents were both that way inclined, my father at London University College, my mother at the LSE, would you believe? All through school, I'd planned on going up to Oxford, reading history, and or classics—finding my bent. My school subjects were heavily weighted that way—no science at all.'

Prue was intrigued by the admission, but left wondering where his path had taken such a turn that he'd ended up where he now was. She was about to ask—was framing the question—when he spoke again.

'I had a friend, right from when I started school. He had cystic fibrosis, had a lot of days off sick. I'd go around to his place after school and tell him what we'd done—try to keep him up with the work.'

Something in his voice told Prue she wasn't going to enjoy this story, but his empathy with the sick child, his willingness to stay friends with the other boy, touched her heart.

'Later, I was to go away to school, but he couldn't so I opted to stay in London. We remained friends.' He paused, turning out to look at the passers-by beyond the potted plants. 'I guess I always knew he was much better after his physio had visited. He had so many, mostly women, but a few men, over the years.'

William was reliving something in his mind—perhaps a particular incident—and Prue could see the pain it caused him in the suddenly deeper shadows on his face.

Then he spun back to face her.

'When my friend died, studying physiotherapy seemed a logical thing to do.'

'It did?' Prue frowned, unable to make the mental leap William must have made to come to this conclusion.

He shrugged his broad, brown-clad shoulders and the smile reappeared, though slightly self-mocking, as if revealing something so personal didn't come easily to him.

'My parents reacted in the same way. Not that they tried to stop me. They just couldn't follow my reasoning.' He paused and she glimpsed remembered sadness in his eyes. 'Perhaps there wasn't any reasoning, any logic, in it, but, at the time, it seemed the right thing to do. The only thing, in fact.'

Prue digested the words, putting herself in the young William's place.

'I can understand that feeling,' she told him. 'You hadn't been able to do much to save your friend suffering, but helping others with the same condition could be your way of paying tribute to him.'

He didn't agree, but nor did he deny her suggestion, moving instead from the personal to the practical.

'It wasn't easy as I had to catch up on all the science stuff before I could begin the course, but somewhere deep inside me the conviction that it was the right choice continued to grow. I've since packed a lot more medical studies into my science Masters, and completed my Masters and doctorate in Physio.'

'Oh, is that all!' Prue said, teasing him with a smile as she realised the amount of study the man had undertaken. 'And here's me complaining about the reading I have to do for my speciality studies!'

'Well, not quite all,' he admitted. His smile teased her right back, sneaking in under her defences and making her feel carefree and relaxed. 'I realised early on I was a better teacher than I was a practitioner. Too easily distracted to be a top-class practising therapist.'

'Did that bother you?'

He seemed taken aback, then the smile widened his lips again and she had to concentrate hard to absorb what he was saying.

'It did at first—made me feel guilty, if you can understand that. But with a little, albeit late-developing, maturity, I realised that by pursuing research I can be just as useful in the fight against, not only CF, but other diseases as well.'

'Does Paediatric Rheumatology fit into your other diseases?' Prue asked, wanting him to keep talking because she liked the conviction she heard in his voice when he spoke of his work—something she guessed went deeper than job satisfaction.

'Not specifically,' he replied. 'Recently I've been sidetracked into this deep muscle research, which should certainly have applications for arthritis sufferers. But cystic fibrosis remains a primary focus. Actually, there's only so much anyone can do to improve the lifestyle of those who suffer it, from a therapy point of view—trialling new exercises, and new massage techniques—so I've a vague long-term goal of research into genetic engineering. More study, and a lot of prac work before I get into that field.'

Prue's smile broadened.

'Well, if dedication counts towards achievement, you

should cure it in the end. Or at least find a way to prevent it in future generations—isn't that the aim of genetic engineering?'

'One of them,' he agreed, then he shook his head. 'But as far as dedication is concerned, in most great medical discoveries, luck played almost as important a part.'

'So, are you lucky?'

It was a light-hearted enough question—asked with a smile. A natural extension of the conversation, she thought. But William looked first startled, and then distinctly puzzled.

He shook his head, as she had so many times earlier in the day when she'd first met him, then frowned as if he couldn't understand what she was saying.

'Can you hear bells?' he demanded, and she listened for a moment.

'It's the little church in Queensberry Mews. Or would sound carry from further along Queen's Gate? The bell-ringers must be practising.'

He frowned at what, to Prue, seemed a quite logical explanation.

'You *can* hear them?' he asked suspiciously. 'You're not just humouring me?'

As the bells stopped ringing at that moment, she wasn't sure what to answer, but fortunately the waitress saved the day, appearing with the dips and a plate of garlicky unleavened bread.

'Did I order the same as you? How boring! We should have made different choices and shared. You should have told me. I lose track of what I'm doing sometimes. Isobel was always very good that way. She'd order for me if I looked like making an error.'

Prue absorbed what she suspected was an example of the man's tumbling thoughts, put into words, perhaps inadvertently. She extracted one sentence.

'You've mentioned Isobel before. Was she your keeper?'

He looked shocked, and then puzzled.

'Did I give that impression? Poor Isobel. I suppose I did use her in much that way at times. We were engaged, you see.'

Prue didn't see at all, but she wanted to, although she had no intention of considering why. She mopped up the last of the beans onto a piece of bread so she didn't appear too eager to know more, then said in a carefully casual voice, 'Engaged?'

'For quite a long time, actually,' William said, as if that made the engagement different in some way. Or his behaviour more acceptable, perhaps.

'How long?' Prue asked.

He hesitated, looking up from his meal to study her face as if it might help his calculations.

'About eight years, I suppose it was,' he said, then he smiled. 'Sounds quite dreadful, put like that. An engagement is supposed to be a pledge to marry, isn't it? A commitment to do something in the near future, not when one gets around to it.'

Their main course arrived, the tang of lemon and hint of subtle spices in the accompanying rice making Prue's mouth water. But not enough to put her off her questions.

'Do I gather you didn't get around to it? What happened to Isobel? Did she die of old age? Sink into a decline while waiting for you to meet her at the altar?'

His eyes twinkled at her.

'She dumped me,' he admitted, looking more delighted than upset by this action. 'Married a car salesman instead.'

Prue went back to her head-shaking routine. The Isobel she'd conjured in her mind had been tall, blonde, elegant and studious—another academic. Hardly the kind of person to take up with a fast-talking car salesman.

'A car salesman?' she echoed faintly, and caught the

crinkling at the corners of William's eyes that told her he was teasing.

'A very superior car salesman,' he assured her. 'Bentleys and such. And, as Isobel snottily pointed out when I showed my surprise, he does own the business!'

Again Prue sensed self-mockery in William's words and she wondered if Isobel's defection had hurt more than he admitted. Not that she had any sympathy for him. A man who let an engagement drag on eight years...

'So now you have no one to order your meals in restaurants,' she mocked. 'Poor you!'

He grinned at her.

'Looking for a job? You're not wearing any rings—does that mean you're unattached? Available?'

He'd turned the teasing back on her, making her feel distinctly uncomfortable.

'Not for meal-ordering,' she said quickly. 'Or to play at being engaged to someone too absent-minded to take the next step, thank you very much.'

She turned her attention to her meal, sliding the cubes of meat off the skewer, then picking up one on her fork.

'You sound like someone who's been there and done that,' he said, and she glanced up, again surprised by his perception. She hadn't let that much emotion show, surely!

'Not really!' she said, shrugging off the question as casually as she could. 'But I've recently made a conscious decision to concentrate on work and studies for a while. No distractions.'

He studied her for a moment, and again she wondered if he read minds, especially when he spoke again.

'No ticking clocks? No worry about not having a family while you're still young? You are still young, aren't you? Twenty-eight? Twenty-nine?'

She chuckled.

'Want my blood group as well? Yes, I'm twenty-eight,

Mr Want-to-know-it-all! And, no, if I've got a biological clock, it certainly isn't ticking. It may never tick, in fact. I love my work. I want to make a career in Paediatric Rheumatology, so I'll always have plenty to do with children.'

'You're saying you don't want children?' Appalled didn't begin to describe his tone.

'You make it sound like a gross character fault!' she muttered. 'And why is it that only women have biological clocks? Why is this ticking business always directed at them?'

'Because men can go on breeding for far longer than women—we can father a child at any age, providing everything remains in working order.'

'Well, bully for you,' Prue muttered, and bent her head to concentrate on her meal.

William saw a frown pucker the skin between his companion's dark eyebrows and wondered why she was so touchy on the subject of children. And why she'd made a 'conscious' decision?

Change the subject, common sense suggested, although he wanted to know more—to know why.

And whether it was set in concrete.

Perhaps it was no more of a commitment to her than his engagement to Isobel had been to him.

But he could hardly pursue it right now when she'd so obviously cut off that discussion!

'So, tell me what the unit does for clients—in a general, more non-medical way. Although I've spent time there before, I've just come and gone, done my therapy sessions and never really delved into the workings of it as a total entity. If Mark and I are to come up with something useful, I need to understand the "big picture"!'

He said the last two words with an exaggerated American accent and was pleased to see Prue smile.

'As far as ancillary stuff goes, we put out a two-monthly newsletter. Claire handles that.'

'How appropriate. Did you know ancillary means ''pertaining to a handmaiden''?'

Again he saw Prue's brow wrinkle, this time in confusion, he guessed.

'I'm sorry! I ask you a question then distract you with trivia. Bad tendency to say whatever pops into my head, though I do try to curb it. Go on.'

She frowned again, as if she had to regather her thoughts after the interruption, then continued.

'We try to organise care coordination, especially for children who have to travel long distances to the hospital. If a child has to see an ophthalmologist, for example, we make that appointment as well, so everything can be done on the same day.'

He nodded, but although he was taking in what she said, and was definitely interested, he was also distracted by the way her lips moved as she spoke, and the little lilt in her voice as she finished a sentence.

You need to get out more, his sensible voice advised. This woman is not interested in a relationship—remember!

'We also have a parent support network, where parents of recently diagnosed children can be put in touch with someone going along, or who has been along, the same path of tests and treatment.'

Even talking shop, her voice beguiled him, blotting out the sensible inner warnings—making him fancy he could hear bells again.

Which was ridiculous!

'And of course there are the usual hospital-provided services, assisted transportation if required, interpreters, lodging for parents whose child is hospitalised. Are you listening to me or am I babbling on while you design another spreadsheet or ponder some obscure genetic code for cystic fibrosis?'

The edge of sarcasm shook him out of his mental musings, although he could still hear those damn bells.

He looked cautiously around, and spotted the child, only a toddler, nestled in a pram by his parents' table, waving in his hand a fluffy toy—a buffalo of some kind, or maybe a cow.

'Yes, it must be a cow, it's got a cowbell,' he muttered, then glanced up to find his dinner partner staring at him, blue eyes so wide he knew she must think he'd taken complete leave of his senses.

'I keep hearing bells,' he mumbled, aware this was a totally inadequate explanation but unable to do better without revealing Isobel's ridiculous remark. 'Believe me, I was listening. Parent network, transport assistance, newsletter. No doubt there's also an advocacy organisation parents can join—outside of what the hospital provides.'

But his recitation must have failed to impress, for Prue shook her head at him again—she had a habit of doing that, he realised—and said, 'I can't believe Isobel put up with it for eight years. Was the woman a saint? Was she honoured in the Queen's Birthday List? For services to humanity in keeping a dangerous man like you from being inflicted on the world at large?'

He tried to look hurt, not easy when his lips kept wanting to smile at her gentle mockery.

'I always imagined she thought me perfect!' he said. 'Which is why the car salesman came as something of a shock.'

'I can imagine!' Prue said, her voice as dry as week-old bread. 'And obviously her defection broke your heart and you're hiding your pain beneath that casually brave exterior.'

Now he did smile at her.

'I should be, shouldn't I?' he said, quite startled to realise, now he came to think about it, that he hadn't been
upset. Put out, definitely. Inconvenienced. Even a little
peeved. But certainly not hurt. 'Upset, I mean. Although it
was a while ago—months, in fact.'

'And you've had to order your own dinner in restaurants
for all that time? Poor man!'

He held up his hands in surrender.

'Okay! That's it! Enough of this roasting William, thank
you! Serves me right for sharing such intimate details of
my life with a woman! I might have known all I'd get is
ridicule. Gone are the days when women were truly
women, all listening ears and adoration, hanging on the
jewels of wisdom falling from their master's lips, full of
sympathy for their male companion's pain and anguish.'

Prue chuckled and William found he liked the sound—
so much so he hoped he could make her laugh again.

'You could get a dog to fill that role,' she told him.
'Probably even teach him to order your meals. One bark
for shish kebabs, two for *dolmas*. Now, do you want to
know more about the unit—or are we ready to talk about
communication?' She raised her eyebrows and smiled at
him. 'Isn't that why we're meeting tonight?'

He should have said yes, and steered the conversation
back to work-related subjects, but her smile had coincided
with more bells. He checked the cow-waving child and saw
he was asleep, strained his ears to see if they were playing
something recognisably religious to confirm they came
from the church, but couldn't separate the notes.

He could hardly mention them again. Not when Prue
Valentine already had doubts about his sanity.

CHAPTER FIVE

THEY finished the meal with apple tea, something William hadn't enjoyed since his visits to Turkey in his student days.

'Was Isobel not an adventurous food-orderer?' Prue asked when he mentioned this.

The re-introduction of Isobel's name startled him.

'I've not thought much about it before—I suppose she knew my likes and dislikes, and ordered accordingly.'

He was feeling well fed and relaxed, and knew, without wanting to analyse why, he'd much rather be talking about Prue Valentine than Isobel. But the woman in question had ducked for cover when he'd tried a gentle probe earlier this evening, so perhaps he'd better stick to shop talk.

Or could he combine the two?

'Is General Medical a new rotation for you? I'm in and out of there from time to time but don't remember seeing you.'

'You're in and out of General Medicine? If you're in and out of anywhere at Lizzie's, shouldn't it be orthopaedics where physios are in most demand?'

'You're the one who said conversation was a two-way street,' he reminded her, 'and here you are, answering questions with more questions.'

She shrugged and smiled, and her eyes, dark in the shadowy light, gleamed with wry amusement.

'I was betraying surprise, not avoiding a reply!' she told him. 'Yes, I'm new on the ward, but—'

'What's the connection between physio and the odds-and-ends ward?' He barely waited for her nod, before continuing. 'There's none. But I'm President of the Cystic Fibrosis Trust and as children with CF are often hospitalised in General Medicine, as well as in the chest ward, I'm a regular visitor.'

She studied him for a moment, then said, 'We're not the only children's hospital in London—and what about young adults? Do you visit them as well? I can't imagine how you forgot to get married, when all you've got on your plate is a little teaching, supervising lecturers and student programmes, studying yourself, conducting research, presidenting an organisation, and doing hospital support visits! I don't suppose you're training as an astronaut in your spare time—or do you play professional golf?'

He had to laugh—and the laughter felt good, especially when Prue joined in with her seductive chuckle.

'You forgot special projects like the communication paper and getting you fit!' he reminded her.

'Well, I'll let you off that one,' she replied, so promptly he felt put out.

'No way!' he told her. 'I'm serious about promoting regular exercise among medical professionals. And I'm a great believer in chipping away at things—remember the song about the ant that brought down the rubber-tree plant?'

'No, I don't,' she said, casting him another suspicion-laden look.

'It had high hopes,' he explained, then realised from the blank expression on Prue's face that he hadn't really explained at all. 'The ant did. My mother used to sing it to me. The gist of it was that if you had high hopes, and really worked at what you wanted to do, you could succeed at anything.'

He looked hopefully at his dinner companion, but no light of understanding was illuminating her lovely face, although he thought he caught a flicker of a smile tilting one corner of her lips. Quickly squelched.

'You're really good for a woman's ego, William Alexander,' she said. 'First I'm equated with a horse and walked back to the stables to dry off my sweat, and now I'm likened to an ant! Are all your metaphors animal or insect based?'

'It was the concept, not the ant itself,' he told her stiffly. 'The "anyone can do anything" idea!'

Now she let the smile loose, which should have made him more relaxed, not more uptight.

Well, not exactly uptight, but different—as if all his senses were suddenly on full alert, his awareness sharpened, blood pumping faster through his veins.

'I wonder what they put in apple tea,' she said, and he stared at her, startled by the statement, wondering if perhaps she felt the same and was pondering mind-altering drugs as a possible additive.

'Apples, and a little nutmeg, I'd guess from the taste,' Prue added, although answering her own questions seemed a foolish thing to do. She'd made the comment to divert him from his talk of physical exercise—in particular his 'project' which involved her.

Her companion let out his breath in a huge sigh.

'You know, for a moment there, I thought you might have felt affected by it. As if they'd added pot or something hallucinogenic.'

'Do you feel that way?' she asked, leaning forward to take his hand and feel for his pulse. Concerned for him. 'No wonder you were rabbiting on about ants. Are you all right now?'

Taking his hand had been a mistake. She realised that almost immediately. It was firm and warm and her own fitted so neatly into it, especially when he'd avoided the pulse-taking by the simple expedient of turning his over to imprison her fingers in a strong but gentle clasp.

'We haven't talked much about communication,' she reminded him, while an inner voice suggested she should remove her hand from his.

Like now!

His fingers tightened, as if the synchronicity that had been happening between them since they had first met was back in action.

'I have not been "rabbiting on", as you so inelegantly put it,' he said huffily, while an idle stroking of her fingers robbed the words of offence.

'You haven't been talking about this special project, either,' she pointed out. 'Apart from some idea of a spreadsheet that sent me to sleep just thinking about it.'

His eyes, so darkly brown—mesmeric—scanned her face. Studying her or simply finding somewhere to rest while he was deep in thought?

'Do you have case meetings? Regular get-togethers of all the staff where particular patients are discussed?'

Finding somewhere to rest, apparently!

'Every Friday, but not everyone can get there each week.' She must stop thinking about his eyes, and really should remove her hand. That gentle sliding of his thumb across her palm was sending ripples of reaction deep into her body.

'Perhaps because people know there's another meeting next week, they don't make the extra effort to attend.'

This is strictly business, she told herself, as she heard his logical suggestion. His clasp on her hand was a meaningless gesture. He'd probably forgotten he was doing it. So why couldn't she concentrate?

She made an effort.

'You mean, if the meeting was monthly, and everyone was there, then the discussion notes could be transmitted, in some convenient form, to the primary carer?'

She thought about it, then nodded.

'I guess it could work. It would certainly give the primary care person more detailed information. But our meetings are usually just the team at Lizzie's. The dietitian may occasionally attend if there's something to be discussed, but the orthopaedic surgeon, social worker, and the ophthalmologist usually send a report, rather than coming along themselves. There are time constraints on everyone.'

'Are those reports presented?' he asked.

'Yes! Someone reads them out.'

'Then how about taping the entire discussion—separate tape for each child. Shoot off the tape to the GP—he can always listen to it in his car if he has no other time. Then he takes notes of what he wants from it. That way, he doesn't end up with unnecessary paperwork, but he not only knows what the team is doing, but understands why they're doing it.'

'But we get off track—talk about side issues all the time,' Prue explained, shuddering as she recalled some of the diverse and relatively unrelated topics they sometimes covered at these sessions.

William seemed unfazed. In fact, he smiled.

'Having the sessions taped might keep you all more focussed,' he told her, his grin widening. 'Although, seriously, I think it's the discussion part that would most interest the health professional caring directly for the child.'

He had a point but if it was so simple, why wasn't it already being done? She was too tired to work that out, or search for an objection. Too tired, and too confused by her reactions to the warm hand, tucked so casually around hers.

'We'd better go,' she said, removing her hand and standing up. 'I haven't the mental energy required to concentrate on this.'

He stood up with her, apparently unperturbed by either the removal of her hand or her declaration of departure.

'I spoke to Mark about the cancelled meeting,' he told

her. 'He suggested the coffee shop at seven-thirty in the morning.'

Prue was startled out of her pleasant lethargy.

'At the hospital? At seven-thirty? Forget it! Ask Crystal to represent the therapists. It's my day off, and days off don't begin until at least midday.'

He was counting out change for the bill as she voiced her objections, and, remembering how he'd missed Pat's arrival in the office earlier in the day, she doubted he'd heard.

The bill!

'How much is it? I'll pay half,' she said, fumbling in her handbag for her wallet.

He heard that much, for he looked up and used 'the smile' to full effect.

'You'll do no such thing. I asked you to eat with me. I said I'd pay so you knew where you stood, and that's the end of it.' His lips curled a little higher, the creases in his cheeks deepening as the smile grew mischievous. 'I'm an old-fashioned man, remember!'

She stopped fumbling, her fingers paralysed by the physical effect the man's smiles were having on her. It must be lack of sleep. She never reacted physically to men. Never felt the heart-lurching and pulse acceleration her friends claimed to experience.

Well, not right off! Attraction was something that grew slowly, fostered by mutual interests and respect, liking, and then love. That was how it had been for her with Paul. And before him, with—

Was it Peter or was that word association? There'd been a teenage boyfriend, ten, twelve years in the past—but surely she should be able to remember his name?

'Robert!'

William looked at her, then glanced around. Trust him

to come back to earth just as she remembered and foolishly said the name aloud.

'Was it someone you know walking past or am I so bland you've forgotten my name already?' He gave a little bow and said, 'I'm William. Remember?'

Prue felt heat she hadn't felt since back in Robert's time scald her cheeks.

'I was thinking of something else,' she muttered, then was further disconcerted when William took her hand again, tucked it back into the crook of his arm, and guided her, with great dignity and style, out from the sheltering pot plants and on to the street.

His smile was gentle but no less powerful.

'I'm glad I'm not the only one who has those aberrations.' His voice held laughter in its depths, and Prue found herself relaxing. She was actually enjoying the company of this man, and the feeling of being protected—even her weird inner reactions weren't half bad!

'So, what if I meet with Mark and fill you in on the discussion at lunch-time. I've checked Annette's appointments and midday looks like a good time for our run. Given you're off duty, we might even get to visit the canteen together.'

His manners might make it seem special, but it was work, Prue reminded herself.

Which was okay with her, since she'd already made that decision to concentrate on work until she'd completed her speciality training.

'I suppose I could meet you at twelve,' she agreed reluctantly, and was surprised to feel his chest vibrate in a silent chuckle.

'You really should try to tone down your enthusiasm,' he told her, the laughter rippling again in his voice. 'Might go to a chap's head if you keep overwhelming him like that!'

She wanted to chuckle at his nonsense but sensed if she gave him an inch he'd take a thousand miles.

'I'm only agreeing because it's easier than saying no then having you badger me into it,' she said firmly. 'And because if it will help Mark out, I'm happy to work on the communication problem. That man carries a huge workload with consultancies at other hospitals as well as running the unit at Lizzie's.'

'And you feel sorry for him?' William complained. 'Only a little while ago you made fun of all I do. Not a shred of sympathy did I get from you.'

'I don't know for sure, but I suspect yours is self-inflicted,' Prue countered. 'My guess is you have a tendency to say yes to suggestions before you even consider the implications. Look at this communication thing. You've barely begun to consider it, and you've come up with two possible theories in less than twenty-four hours.'

'It's the way my brain works,' William explained apologetically. 'But you're right. I do tend to bite off more than I can chew.'

'And then what?' Prue asked, enjoying the ebb and flow of the conversation.

'I chew like mad!' he said, and this time she did chuckle.

They walked in harmony the short distance to her block of flats.

'I'm not asking you in,' she told him, just in case he had any false expectations. 'Not because coffee on top of apple tea would be gross, but because I really am very tired.'

He turned his head and looked down into her face, and once again she felt those dark eyes studying her, as if assessing her in some way.

'Sleep well,' he said gently, then, as if in an afterthought, added, 'but we haven't organised anything for tomorrow. Where will I meet you? At the unit at twelve?'

She nodded and retrieved her hand from the warm nook where it had rested.

'Goodnight,' she said, then she ducked away, afraid if she hesitated her lips would open and she'd find herself inviting him in after all. She reached the door and fumbled for her key, then couldn't get it to go in.

'Let me.'

He must have followed her up the steps, and now he took the key from her nerveless fingers, inserted it, and, naturally, unlocked the door with ease. He turned the knob and pushed it open for her, then reached out and touched her cheek.

'Goodnight, wise and cautious Prue,' he murmured.

Now what on earth did he mean by that? she asked herself as she trudged up the central staircase to her flat.

Surely he hadn't expected to be asked in? He couldn't have seen their night out as anything more than a business meeting—could he?

It must be tiredness that had invested the words with disturbing nuances.

Prue woke at six-thirty, feeling as fresh as if she'd slept the clock around. She made a cup of tea and snuggled back into bed, then thought of the young child, Michael, admitted the previous afternoon, and his anxious mother.

If she got up now, she could pop over to the hospital, check on Michael, make the seven-thirty breakfast appointment with Mark, then get an early start on some serious grocery shopping—restocking shelves depleted by too little time off.

Assuring herself that this urge to visit the hospital at the crack of dawn on her day off had nothing whatsoever to do with William Alexander, she eased back out of bed before she became too comfortable, showered and—

Thought about what to wear.

The track suit?

Hardly!

One of the selection of skirts and tops she usually wore to work?

They all seemed drab today—essentially dull and boring, in fact.

A glance at the window revealed London morning gloom although she was reasonably sure the weather bureau had promised sunshine later. Still, a summer dress might be optimistic, not to mention foolhardy.

This is ridiculous! she muttered to herself. The man is nothing more than a colleague—nor are you any more than that to him.

She pulled out her trusty jeans that had stretched enough to be really comfortable. Took one look at their baggy shape and thrust them back into the cupboard, seeking instead the new stretch jeans she'd bought at an 'end of summer' sale the previous year.

They were a pale butter-yellow, and in a moment of madness she'd bought a cotton knit sweater to go with them. It had a white background with a pattern of blue and butter-yellow flowers across it. Alive, but not too bright, a one-off design that had originally been priced on a par with a night at the Ritz, but reduced to almost affordable levels thanks to the sale.

Excitement fluttered in her stomach as she dressed, but she knew that was natural. She so rarely 'got dressed up' these days, putting on anything new was exciting.

Or so she told herself as she smoothed a fine film of foundation across her cheeks, adding a touch of blusher, a hint of blue to her eyelids, mascara—not too much—and a soft pink lip gloss.

'Mmm, you smell nice,' Robyn Devlin, the sister on duty at the ward greeted her.

Prue was glad she'd buttoned her white coat over the sweater—to look dressed up as well as smelling good would have been a dead give-away to the staff on the ward.

'I'm on a day off. Just popped in to see Michael,' she explained.

Robyn waved her towards the bed.

'Good thing you're early. Mark's just been to see him and they're packing up to go home. I think they've an appointment at the unit for later in the week.'

Prue was puzzled. Mark often kept young children in hospital when they began anti-inflammatory medication to monitor possible adverse reactions.

'Dad's a nurse,' Robyn explained, correctly guessing at the question in Prue's mind. 'He's taken time off so he can attend the first clinic visit and is happy to monitor the drugs.'

'Good for him,' Prue said. 'I do wish more fathers would take an interest in their children's treatment. I know it's difficult when most of them work full-time—but a lot of mothers work the same hours these days, yet they still manage to fit in the ''family'' type extras.'

'I've been telling my husband that for years,' Robyn said. 'And when I see how Holly has Ben trained to help around the house I could spit.'

'Ben had two good reasons in Beth and James to become more domesticated,' Prue reminded her. 'And some men might be easier to train than others.'

But even as she spoke her mind shot off at a tangent, wondering about the trainability—or otherwise—of William.

He'd be impossible! she told herself. He might have good intentions, but whether household tasks could hold his attention for long enough to get them finished, she doubted.

She crossed to Michael's bed, and found, as Robyn had predicted, the child ready to go home.

'It was really very comfortable, staying here the night,' Maureen Leski told her. 'I was surprised at how caring everyone was, and how at home they made me feel. And Michael slept right through.'

'Probably a hangover of sedation from the anaesthetic,' Prue told her. 'You're coming back to visit us in the clinic later in the week?'

Maureen nodded.

'Brian, my husband, he told me last night that he'd been worried about it being leukaemia or bone cancer. He hadn't stopped to think about arthritis, but now he knows he says that's much better, and although it will be a drag, we'll manage. He hadn't mentioned cancer to me because he didn't want me fretting over it, just told me over the phone the other night to bring Michael to the hospital, and he'd be back as soon as he could.'

Prue followed the explanation without much difficulty. Relief was a fairly typical reaction when parents were told their child was suffering one or other form of childhood rheumatics. Cancer was such a huge fear, anything less ominous than that was acceptable.

'It will still be hard for you—for all of you,' she warned Maureen. 'Michael will have periods of bad pain. You'll have to exercise his joints and muscles every day. He'll need more of your attention than the other children, which could lead to some of them feeling left out—even resentful of Michael's demands on your time.'

Michael, who was playing with an obviously well-loved rabbit, glanced up at that moment and smiled.

Prue reached out and gently ruffled his hair.

'Seems impossible, doesn't it, little one, that anyone could be jealous of time spent with you? You are so cute.'

'Do you have children of your own?'

Prue shook her head. The hollow sensation in the pit of her stomach was definitely not regret. And the ticking noise she could hear was probably the central heating turning on or off.

She changed the subject, asking about the projected clinic visit, warning Maureen they could be there for some hours as Mark would undoubtedly line up a number of specialists to see Michael.

They chatted for a while longer, and when Brian Leski arrived to take his wife and youngest child home, Prue excused herself and left.

'You're not here to work?' Robyn asked as she ducked past the desk.

'Not today,' Prue told her. 'Even junior dogsbodies get a day off occasionally.'

'Enjoy it!' Robyn called after her, and Prue smiled to herself as she realised that she possibly would. The beginning of it, anyway. Once she got to the shopping part—a task she hated—and the studying part that would come later, it would be as predictable as most of her days off.

Mark was already in the coffee shop, head bent over a sheaf of papers. He glanced up as Prue joined him, and nodded to her.

'Good. I'm glad you're here. Crystal's doing a home visit today so couldn't make it. And something else has come up.'

'Now why does that sound ominous?' Prue asked, shifting her chair to make more room at the table when she saw William walk in.

'Because it is!' Mark grumbled. 'I know we're part of the hospital, and I do appreciate the ongoing commitment of the money men to the unit, but they just don't realise how poorly staffed we are compared to other areas.'

William settled himself comfortably at the table, shifting

his chair slightly so the gap Prue had manoeuvred between her chair and his narrowed again.

He'd nodded and smiled at her as he'd sat down, apparently not at all surprised to find her there. He then bent all his attention to what Mark was saying, although Prue doubted he'd understand it any better than she could.

'I've often wondered about your staffing situation,' William said as Mark paused to sip at his lethal looking black coffee. 'Are the staff paid by the hospital or does the unit run on a special grant or budget?'

'Hospital paid,' Mark replied gloomily. 'That's why Prue here has to combine ward work with her time at the unit. Admin inisists she work the house officers' full complement of hours!'

'And is it Prue's roster that's bothering you at the moment?' William asked, and Mark looked surprised.

'Prue's roster?' He glanced towards Prue. 'I rarely know what days or times she's on duty. She always turns up on time for clinic sessions and I bleep her if I need her at other times, but she's slotted into hospital routine for most of her working hours.'

William turned to Prue and raised his eyebrows as if to say, Well, if it's not you, what's bothering him?

Prue shrugged and held out her hands. William's brown eyes were no less beguiling at breakfast than they'd been in the lamplight at the restaurant the previous evening.

'So, what's worrying you, Mark?' William asked the obvious.

'It's the bloody Easter Egg Hunt!' Mark said bitterly. 'Apparently someone told me about it weeks ago. Not only told me, but reminded me that it was the unit's turn to take on the organisation of a "Special Event".'

He wiggled his fingers in the air to give the final two words inverted commas.

'Organisation rotates,' he said by way of explanation to

William. 'Who did the Fancy Dress Ball, Prue? Was it A and E?'

'I can't remember, but I'm sure William gets the idea. I take it the rotation has reached us and we're on for the Easter festivities. It's for the patients, not a fund-raising function, so we've no outside committee involved. Shouldn't be too bad.'

Mark glared at her.

'How can you say that? Of course it will be too bad! What on earth do any of us know about Easter Egg Hunts?'

Prue chuckled.

'You must have had them when you were young. Some kindly adult hides the Easter eggs and all the kids look for them.'

'Great!' Mark groaned. 'Can't you imagine all the mobile kids at Lizzie's tearing up and down the corridors, or skating along on their drip stands, searching for Easter eggs? It would be pandemonium.'

Subduing her chuckle to a smile, Prue moved to calm him.

'Absolute bedlam,' she agreed. 'It will have to be organised. Perhaps a real hunt—like a treasure hunt—with clues. Kids who can't get out of bed could follow it in some way—perhaps on paper like a snakes and ladders game.'

Mark stared at her.

'It's the organisation I'm objecting to,' he pointed out. 'I simply don't have time.'

'I do,' William said, and Prue smiled again.

'I knew you'd be like that,' she reminded him. 'Mark hasn't even called for volunteers and your hand's already up. Don't you have enough going on in your life already?'

'Most probably,' he agreed gravely. 'But I can never resist a challenge. Besides, I'll be interested to see exactly how you plan to organise your hunt on paper for the children who can't get out of bed.'

'Me organise it?' Prue stuttered. 'I didn't volunteer—you did. I was just throwing out ideas.'

'And very good ideas they were too,' Mark said. 'Now that's settled—you and Will are in charge of the Easter Egg Hunt—perhaps we could get down to real work.' He hesitated and looked up from the paper he'd been studying, to say, 'Draft in anyone else you need, and Claire has a copy of the budget the hospital has allocated.'

I can't shake my head again, Prue told herself, quelling the gesture with difficulty.

Not that head-shaking would help. Having issued his command, Mark had moved on and was already listening to William explain his idea of taping the case meetings.

'It could work,' Mark said, staring into space as his mind pondered the idea. 'What about litigation? Is there any chance we could get into strife for saying something untoward? I mean, if it goes to another medico, and is kept with the patient file, then how can we be sure a patient's family never got access to it?'

'There'd have to be an understanding by the recipient that notes are taken from it then the tape destroyed. Or perhaps returned to the unit to be re-used,' Prue suggested. 'And it's not as if we trash our patients. Most of our discussions are very positive.'

'Except when Annette's complaining that a parent's being slack about the exercise routine,' Mark reminded her. 'And I've heard you voice a suspicion that medication is sometimes forgotten in certain households.'

'But isn't that the kind of comment you want your hands-on doctor to hear? Isn't that what he or she should know?' William asked. 'After all, they see the family more often, and can chivvy them if necessary. Keep an eye on things at a more local level.'

'There's something in that,' Mark agreed, then he broke off to order a very unhealthy breakfast of bacon and eggs.

Prue resisted a cholesterol overload, and ordered fruit compote and a muffin.

'Very sensible,' William told her, ordering muesli for himself, and echoing her request for a fruit muffin. 'And see what I mean about the general state of health in the medical profession?'

He nodded significantly in Mark's direction, then shared a conspiratorial smile with Prue.

'I'm not going to change my eating habits for you, Will Alexander, so give over,' Mark grumbled. 'Although, I must admit, the month I spent in the US last year very nearly stopped me ordering bacon and eggs for ever. Do you know the Americans have about eight varieties of eggs, and every morning you have to make a choice of which one you want?'

'Muesli's muesli wherever you go, although I'll admit some is better than others,' William told him. 'You should try it some time.'

'I have tried it. Anna lives on the stuff. And speaking of Anna, when I told her you were back with us, she insisted I ask you to a staff do we're having Saturday night. Her idea, of course. She says I'm not kind enough to them so every now and then she likes to put on something special. Isobel still around? Bring her along if you like.'

Prue glanced at William and read the uncertainty in his face. Maybe Isobel's defection had hurt him more than he was willing to admit. Was that why he didn't want to tell Mark about it?

The silence lengthened and she was about to break it by shifting the conversation back to the subject of taping their case meetings when William spoke.

'Isobel can't make it, but if you're going, Prue, maybe we could go together. Save taking two cars out to Wimbledon.'

'An eminently sensible plan,' Mark agreed, then he

added plaintively, 'So now we've sorted out your social lives, could we get back to work?'

Sorted out your social lives? Whose social lives?

Hers and William's?

No way!

CHAPTER SIX

'How far have you got with the GPs?' William asked Mark, switching the conversation with his usual dexterity. 'You were going to contact all those involved with the children at the unit to find out what works and what doesn't in the current situation.'

Mark thanked the waitress who'd just delivered his hearty breakfast before turning back to William.

'I must confess I'm a bit behind with that although Claire has it in hand now. We're sending reply-paid envelopes so with any luck we'll be getting the first answers in next week.'

'Until we know what the doctors out there want in the way of information, it's a bit hard to proceed, isn't it?' Prue suggested.

William was pouring milk onto his muesli but Mark looked up at her.

'While I've got Will on hand to jump-start ideas, we might as well develop some theoretical plans. We can adapt and modify them later, to fit in with what's required. I'll talk to someone in the legal department about the pitfalls of taped sessions—it would have to be with the patient's or family's consent, of course.'

They discussed the pros and cons of the taping idea, and William talked about some form of simple spreadsheet. Prue actually followed what he was saying that time, and realised there could be benefits in it, if the idea was refined.

Unperturbed by William's disapproval of his eating habits, Mark tackled his breakfast with gusto, slicing bacon into neat pieces then putting down his knife, American-style, to fork it into his mouth. And in between, he kept the conversation flowing. Ideas were tossed back and forth, some to be considered later, while others were discarded.

'You might check with Claire, Prue, about the status of the queries to GPs, then collate the information that comes in,' Mark suggested, when his plate had been cleared away. 'Pass on anything relevant to Will.'

He glanced up at William, then looked at Prue.

'You're both happy about working on this together? It's not urgent in the sense that there's no deadline for the paper. The Easter business is another matter, but, as you both volunteered for that, I assume you have enough spare time to get something sorted.'

'I did not volunteer for it,' Prue reminded him, but her healthy breakfast had filled her with such a sense of well-being her protest held little heat.

'Well, someone volunteered you,' Mark said. The bacon and eggs consumed, he was now spreading marmalade thickly on a piece of toast. 'See, no butter, Will. You can't say that's not healthy eating!'

William shuddered theatrically.

'I'm not going to think about the number of calories in half an inch of marmalade,' he said. 'You're a throwback to days past, Mark Gregory!'

'Me a throwback?' Mark joked. 'When you're the original antediluvian man?' He popped the last morsel of toast into his mouth, finished his coffee, and stood up. 'Well, children, I must love you and leave you. Duty calls. I assume you're not working today, Prue, that you're dressed like the embodiment of spring. Thank you for making time this morning. Enjoy your day off.'

He walked briskly away.

'Embodiment of spring, indeed,' Prue muttered, surprised Mark had noticed what she was wearing, and disconcerted that he'd mentioned it. She didn't want William Alexander thinking she'd dressed especially for him.

'Well, you do. And very nice it is too,' William told her. 'Are you doing something special after breakfast? Going somewhere nice?'

Did Sainsbury's count as nice?

Or, dressed up, should she shop at Fortnum and Mason's?

'I didn't think you were coming this morning. Didn't expect to see you until lunch-time,' William continued.

Perhaps he hadn't expected a reply to his questions.

'But now you're here and I've a little time to spare, do you have any ideas about this Easter business? I don't get many chances to do something like this for hospitalised children, so let's make it special.'

'It's like being swept along on a roller coaster, this association with you,' Prue told him. 'I don't want anything to do with "this Easter business" as you call it, and how could I have any ideas when it's just been sprung on me thirty minutes ago?'

'But you mentioned a treasure hunt—that's an idea,' William reminded her.

'That was an idle remark—not a real idea. I mean, I haven't a clue how something like that would work.'

He smiled at her, and she suddenly knew why she'd woken so early in the morning, and why her old blue jeans had looked so drab and shapeless. William's smiles had bewitched her.

No relationships, no complications—*no men*, she reminded herself. Not until you've finished your studies.

If then!

Bewitchment was definitely out!

'We could run it over a week, maybe two. Clue is the operative word. Daily clues, perhaps. Colours for the younger children, riddles for the older ones. Work it as a ward thing. How would that go?'

'I haven't the faintest idea what you're talking about,' Prue said crossly. 'And Easter is less than three weeks away, so if you run something over a fortnight, that only gives us a matter of days to organise it. Couldn't we just have a rabbit hop around the wards handing eggs out of his basket?'

He gave her a look that suggested the idea was unworthy of comment.

'You're right about not having much time. I'm afraid I've got to cry off lunch, something's come up at the university. Then I've a lecture I can't avoid at seven. We can talk as we run later today, I can fit that in, but for a really solid session of brainstorming, could we meet for coffee at nine? Would that suit you?'

'Nine tonight?' The words came out as a high-pitched squeak of disbelief. 'Are you serious about this? About planning something special? At such short notice? And with the workload you're already carrying, not to mention Mark's project, and getting me fit—'

He used the smile to full effect, cutting her off mid-objection.

'I haven't even got to why I can't do it,' she grumbled. 'But if we have to meet, then nine's fine with me. Could we make it my place? Flat four, first floor on the left of the landing. If the door doesn't open after you've pressed the buzzer, buzz again and I'll come down.'

'You're talking like someone who won't see me at midday. We've a date, remember?' Dark eyes twinkled into hers, making remembering anything very difficult.

'Running around the park with someone is hardly a date,' she managed to reply.

She was so adamant, William again wondered whether she'd recently been hurt by someone. Dressed in civvies, she was even more attractive than she'd been in the white coat the previous morning, and she had intelligence, not to mention a sense of fun, that combined to make her a lively and challenging companion.

A man would have to have been a fool to turn away from her. Or turn her away from him.

He smiled, mainly to hide the uneasiness the thought of her in pain caused him.

'So it's not a date,' he agreed. 'And I don't suppose you'd count our going together to Mark's place on Saturday night as anything more than convenience?'

She did the eye-widening trick again as she looked at him.

'Why are we discussing dates?' she demanded. 'We've less than three weeks to Easter, a paper to prepare, you're probably due at work, and I need to shop.'

'Ah, so that explains the classy clothes,' he said, teasing her because he liked the way her eyes sparkled when she took a bait. 'Harrods Food Hall, no doubt.'

She didn't take it after all, but chuckled instead, the sound he found so delightful combining with a ringing noise.

Not again!

He needed a hearing check.

Tinnitus—that was what it must be.

'Is that you being bleeped or me?' she asked, pulling the tiny transmitter that was the curse of all doctors out of her handbag.

'I refuse to carry one so it must be you,' William told her, relieved to find the bells he'd heard were nothing more than her message machine. Feeling puzzled as to why someone would hurt Prue Valentine was a very different matter from hearing bells in his head when she chuckled.

Not that he believed the bell nonsense.

'I've a group therapy session with the under fives this

morning,' he said, turning the subject firmly back to work-related topics.

But Prue wasn't listening, her attention on the message on the screen of her pager.

'It's Mark,' she said, when she'd tucked it back into her handbag. 'He's bleeped me hoping you'd still be here. He wants to talk to you before your therapy session.'

William checked the time and realised he'd have to go. He refused to analyse the sense of disappointment he felt.

'I'll see you later,' he said, pushing back his chair. 'Sorry to abandon you like this.'

Prue waved him away.

'Think nothing of it,' she said. 'I'll even pay for your breakfast. Not quite fair exchange for you paying for our dinner last night, but a token gesture.'

'You can't do that,' he protested, feeling automatically for his wallet.

She reached out and touched his hand, stopping the movement dead.

'Of course I can, antediluvian man,' she said gently. 'Now off you go before he comes looking for you.'

He stared at her, bemused by both the intimacy of the gesture, and what sounded like tenderness in her voice.

And by his reaction to both!

'I'll see you later,' he muttered, then realised he was repeating himself and beat a hasty retreat from the coffee shop.

At least no bells had rung when she'd touched him—although the patch of his skin where her fingers had rested was still tingling slightly.

Not that Isobel had mentioned tingly skin as part of a true romantic's reactive processes.

'I'm concerned about Marcie Wells, one of the children you'll see this morning.' Mark's remark as William walked into his office brought him out of his consideration of tingling and romanticism.

'Concerned in what way? To do with therapy practices?' Mark was frowning over the file on his desk.

'You could put it that way,' he said. 'I've only met the parents a couple of times, when Marcie was first diagnosed. An au pair brings her to appointments and therapy sessions.' He looked up, and William read indecision in his eyes.

Then the specialist nodded, as if having made a decision.

'Annette saw bruises on the child's limbs last time she was here. Inga, the au pair, said the arthritis had made Marcie clumsy and she was always bumping into things but I'm wary of glib answers.'

William felt a tightness in his chest, and forced himself to breathe deeply. He knew his immediate reaction of rage to even such a vague unvoiced suggestion of child abuse was primitive and had to be brought under control.

'I'll take special note,' he promised. 'Maybe get the au pair to help with exercises. Would she be the one doing them for and with the child?'

'I would say so,' Mark told him. 'Both parents are lawyers and you know the hours the young lions in that profession have to work. Almost as bad as doctors!'

William controlled another rush of heat. No parent should be too busy to notice bruises on their child.

He made his way reluctantly to the room where group therapy sessions were held. Crystal was already there, a range of toys set out on a big table.

'Toy library,' she explained. 'I lend out according to the child's needs at the time. Saves parents buying expensive toys that a child might only need or use for a few months. This lot here are good for developing fine motor skills—' she indicated a selection of gaily coloured posting boxes and toys with switches and keys on them '—while these are great for mobility—push-along things for a child who's almost walking, and noisy pull-alongs for those who've taken off and want everyone to know about it.'

William selected one of the posting boxes and turned it over in his hands, imagining toys in primary colours scattered around his flat, a chubby baby crawling towards one of these spheres.

'I must be going daft,' he said to Crystal. 'Not even in Isobel's and my most romantic moments did I think about children, so why should I be broody now?'

She patted her stomach.

'Maybe it's the company you're keeping,' she teased. 'I know before I became pregnant I'd often look with envy at a pregnant woman.'

She studied him for a moment, then added, 'Although I wouldn't have thought that would work for men. It was a physical thing with me, like a hormonal nudge.'

A hormonal nudge!

Was that what was happening to him?

Not that men had hormones the way women did—well, they certainly *had* a full complement of them, but the men he knew didn't consider them responsible for their moods or feelings. Definitely not.

While he, himself, had always considered intellectual attraction, a matching of minds, a far greater rush than the mechanical responses of his body to an attractive female.

'Though I've never actually tingled before!' he mused.

'What *are* you talking about?' Crystal demanded, and he came back down to earth with a thud.

'Therapy ideas!' he muttered, although the gleam in her pretty eyes suggested she suspected the lie. 'Do you stay?'

'Not always but I'd like to observe today if that won't bother you. Seeing them doing their exercises in a group like this can sometimes give me ideas of extra supports they might need. On a one to one basis, they tend to try harder, so I miss wrist or finger weakness that could be helped by either a splint or a modified implement.'

William wondered if Mark had mentioned Marcie Wells to Crystal, and if her presence was to add an extra observer to the room. Not that he could ask—patient confidentiality was so touchy a subject, it was better to say nothing.

The children began to arrive, some leaving their adult hand-holder quite happily and settling on the brightly patterned rug Crystal had spread on the floor in the centre of the room. Others had to be coaxed to separate, but eventually he had six wary-eyed youngsters looking up at him.

Pat, who'd come in with the first arrivals, introduced him, then settled into a chair by the table with her pile of files, and the small tape player William had asked her to bring along.

He squatted down on the rug, cursing a lack of flexibility that made cross-legged sitting very awkward. And wearing something more flexible than a three-piece suit might have been a good move. When he'd dressed this morning he'd been thinking of a meeting in the early afternoon, not playing singing games.

He ran through in his mind the musical programme he'd planned, a sing-along with a lot of clapping and finger-clicking to begin, then more active movement of limbs and arms in songs involving trains and animals, finishing up with a hokey-cokey.

Unless…

'We're going to have a singing day today. Who can sing?'

Small hands shot into the air, and William nodded to Pat to start the tape.

The children joined in with gusto, but William found it easy to detect which joints were either stiff or painful.

'Isn't it sad that your mums and dads or the friends who brought you are missing out on all this fun?' he asked, when they'd finished a particularly lively rendition of Heads and Shoulders, Knees and Toes.

Six small heads nodded, and William turned to the group of adults, sitting along one side of the room.

'Come and join us,' he suggested. 'I know you might see this as your time off, but I've copies of this tape, and you might find with the little ones it makes exercising easier. For instance, the next song is "Dorothy's Dance Party".' He turned to the children. 'Who knows that one?'

'It's the Wiggles,' one brave soul replied. 'I like the Wiggles. Did you know they are from Australia?'

'Yes, and I like them too,' William told the little girl.

The adults moved forward.

'Kneeling behind your charge would be best,' he suggested, 'because the children have to stand up for this one.' He focussed his attention back on the children. 'I'll do the actions first for those of you who don't know it, then you'll all join in the second time with your big person helping you do the actions.'

He performed the simple dance routine in time to the music, and all the children clapped at his exaggerated antics. When everyone joined in, he kept singing and dancing with the music, but, unobtrusively he hoped, observed Marcie and Inga more particularly than the others.

'That was great,' he said, when the song finished and everyone flopped back down onto the floor to rest. 'Now, Mums and Dads and carers, although this session has therapeutic value for the children, it should also be fun. In addition to daily exercises, which are often not fun at all, these singing and dancing games can provide a range of mobility which achieve good results without the stress.'

'Tyrone's knee is that bad usually I didn't think he'd stand up, but he was dancing there with the other kids,' one woman agreed. 'Can we do it instead of his exercises?'

Always a risk, William thought, but didn't say.

'Would you like to run through Tyrone's exercises—not full sets, just one of each—and I'll be able to tell you which could be covered by the tape?'

Tyrone gave a long-suffering sigh that made him seem forty instead of four, but lay obediently on his back and waited for his mother to demonstrate their daily exercise regimen.

'Use the dancing as an extra,' William told her when he realised dancing wasn't the answer to all Tyrone's problems. 'But perhaps if Tyrone has the tape, and knows he'll be dancing later in the day, he'll try harder with his exercises so his dancing will get better. Especially the high kicks, Tyrone.'

Tyrone beamed at him and William found himself beaming back. The kid was so cute—so appealing. He glanced up at the clock, although he knew he had plenty of time. Surely he hadn't heard it ticking.

'Now, who else? You're a good dancer, Marcie,' he said, leaning closer to the little girl. 'How about you show me the exercises you do at home? I bet you're good at them.'

If he hadn't been watching he would have missed the flicker of apprehension in her eyes before she gave a slow nod of assent. Inga had no such hesitation, moving Marcie into the centre of the circle of children and pushing her, not harshly but with unnecessary briskness, onto her back.

William was immediately sorry he'd asked, aware of what was about to happen and desperately sorry he was putting the child through more misery. Inga wasn't cruel, nor even deliberately unfeeling. She was enthusiastic, and an obvious believer in the theory that if a little will do you good, a lot will do you even better.

As William's stomach knotted, his only consolation was that the brisk approach meant the ordeal was over very quickly. Marcie hadn't whimpered or objected and, as far as he could see, the other carers present had noticed nothing untoward.

But he'd seen the whitening of Marcie's skin where Inga's strong fingers gripped, and the red marks where bruises could later appear.

He moved quickly on to more singing games and the final hokey-cokey was a hilarious jumble of limbs going every which way. Inga performed the dance with the same gusto she'd used on Marcie's exercise. It was her nature causing the problem rather than deliberate cruelty, William decided, especially when he saw her as the session ended, picking up the little girl and cuddling her with a tenderness that belied her earlier actions.

But how to approach the subject of less forceful manipulation?

He made general comments to all the adults about using soft fingers when manipulating a child's limbs, talked about bone structure not fully set and the risk of greenstick fractures.

But his mind continued to play with the specific problem of Marcie's exercise routine while he spoke to the other parents, mentioning small weaknesses he'd picked up, areas where some extra therapy might be needed. Pat took notes of his advice, although he knew he'd remember it later, a habit of association helping his mind keep the matters he wanted recorded clear in his head.

'Ah, Inga. How long have you been with Marcie and her family?'

'One year now,' she said, her accent strong but the words precise. Possibly everything would be precise where Inga was concerned.

'Does Marcie have an individual appointment soon?' he asked. 'There are a few minor details I'd liked to talk to Dr Gregory about before changing them in her routine.'

Inga shook her head.

'She came last week, next appointment in three weeks.'

'Would you be able to bring her if I can arrange something sooner?' William asked.

Inga nodded her agreement with the same enthusiasm she'd used for dancing, then she smiled coyly at William, fluttered her eyelashes, and said, 'Any time.'

Crystal materialised by his side.

'I've some toys that might suit Marcie, Inga,' she said. 'So when you've finished...'

'I'll get Claire to fix up an appointment and let Marcie's parents know,' William told Inga and was rewarded by another dazzling smile. 'And in the meantime,' he added, wanting to spare the child more discomfort, 'forget the exercises and just do the singing and playing routines. Let Marcie move naturally, not with you helping her.'

'I thought I should head Inga off,' Crystal said to him later, when they met up in the office at the end of the morning's work. 'I think flirting comes naturally to her and, after the way you couldn't take your eyes off her throughout the session, I guess she thought you were interested.'

She paused, then frowned. 'Heavens! That sounds awful. Perhaps you were. Interested, I mean. She *is* very attractive.'

Stunned by Crystal's garbled conversation—not to mention her assumptions—he couldn't answer straight away. Behind him the office door had opened and then closed, but Pat was adding fuel to Crystal's fire and whoever had walked in was the least of his worries.

'I considered ringing time out and reminding him about professional-patient relationships,' Pat said, chuckling at her own humour as she teased him. 'Talk about knocked out!'

'Who was knocked out and by whom?' a soft, familiar voice asked, and William felt as if he'd stepped into a nightmare.

'The beautiful Inga has knocked our Prof for six!' Pat replied, and William spun to face Prue, wanting to explain to her, not to the stupid females who'd started this nonsense.

'I was watching her for a particular reason,' he protested, dismayed by the caution he read in her lovely blue eyes. 'Mark asked—'

He stopped, realising it wasn't caution, but understanding and concern.

'Give over, girls,' Prue said. 'I'm not denying he might be lusting after the gorgeous au pair, but I know Mark was going to ask him to observe Inga's technique.'

She raised her dark, arced eyebrows at him, asking for confirmation. He nodded, and the sudden stillness in the room suggested Pat and Crystal either knew or suspected something was amiss with Marcie Wells.

'Oh, gosh! I'd forgotten about the bruises,' Crystal said. 'We talked about it at the last case meeting. Inga seems so fond of Marcie I'd ruled her out as a possibility.'

'Could she be so fond she pushes the child too far?' William asked, relieved the subject was out in the open now, but a little concerned that Prue might still imagine he'd be attracted to the buxom blonde. 'I think that's all it is and have suggested we set up an appointment as soon as possible.'

'With the parents?' Prue asked.

William looked at her and wondered why anyone could assume he found Inga's blonde beauty appealing when this dark-headed sprite was jostling the hormones he didn't want to admit to having.

He shut his eyes in denial of hormonal urges, and brought his mind back to the subject of their discussion.

'It's the communication thing again, isn't it? I don't know what Mark will want to do, but it seems to me it's the parents' responsibility to see the child is protected from physical abuse whether it's deliberate or unintentional. And if health professionals who see the child once a month have observed a problem, then why haven't the parents picked up on it?'

'You're saying speak to the parents, not to Inga?' Crystal asked.

'I think so,' William answered, thinking through a process as he spoke. 'And teach one or both of the parents the correct techniques for exercise and ask them to supervise until they are satisfied Inga has it right.'

'I think that would be best for another reason, as well,' Prue put in. 'After all, if Inga's to continue to bring Marcie for appointments, it's better she's not offside with the team here.'

William smiled at her.

'Makes my being here serendipitous, wouldn't you say? If any resentment is felt, Inga can direct it at me, so the rest of the team can continue to work amicably, if warily, with her.'

A smile is a simple movement of muscles and rearrangement of lips, Prue told herself. It is not an electric charge, or a cattle prod, so it shouldn't send your nerves into a frenzy of tingling reaction.

'—agree?'

She missed whatever Crystal was saying, but, as Pat made some reply, maybe the conversation hadn't been directed at her.

'I'd better go and change,' she muttered, thinking a brisk walk to the washroom might restore order to her embattled body.

'Change? Into what?' Crystal demanded. 'You're looking so gorgeous in that outfit I thought you must have a hot lunch date.'

Prue grinned at her.

'Change into my track suit,' she replied. 'I do have a

lunch date—it's for a jog around the park. Be thankful your condition precludes this obsessive man from including you in his make-medical-personnel-fitter campaign.'

She turned to Pat.

'You're not pregnant, and you're medical staff—why isn't he hassling you?'

Pat laughed.

'He has tried, from time to time, but gave up on me as a bad job. And be thankful he's stuck to running with you. One year when he was here, he had the whole unit doing water aerobics in the pool. Not a pretty sight, I can assure you.'

'I thought you were having fun,' William said plaintively to Pat, then he nodded to Prue. 'Well, off you go to change. I can't be hanging around here all day waiting for you.'

Prue looked him up and down.

'And you're running in a three-piece suit?'

She left the rooms to the sound of delighted female laughter, and William's deeper voice tripping over words as he tried to untangle himself from the situation.

CHAPTER SEVEN

It was another glorious day, the usual winds of late March having given way to spring. The daffodils nodded in a slight breeze which also sent scattered showers of blossom drifting downwards from the trees.

'This weather won't last,' Prue reminded William, puffing along beside him as he upped the pace from a brisk walk to a gentle jog. 'We do have the day off when it rains, don't we?'

He turned to grin at her.

'Praying for rain, are you?'

She shook her head, all she could manage as the puffing became panting, and speaking impossible.

But when all was said and done, she *did* want to get fit. And being bullied into it was probably the only way she'd achieve that goal.

'We could swim,' he suggested, 'although at this time of the year, I run in the rain as well. It's not too cold, and the rain is more a drizzle than a torrential downpour. The umbrella looks a bit odd, but we English are supposed to be oddities so I don't let it bother me.'

She stopped running because she had to question this statement—and see his face as she did so.

'You run with an umbrella?'

His eyes were puzzled as they met her gaze.

'Why ever not?'

Prue shook her head and started running again.

Why ever not?

The man was mad, but, try as she might, she couldn't think of a reason for *not* running with an umbrella.

Although there was no way—repeat, no way—she told herself firmly, that she'd be caught dead doing something so ridiculous.

'What about a ward-by-ward thing, so each clue leads to a particular ward where the next clue is concealed—or perhaps will be revealed at a set time?'

She hauled her mind back from aerodynamic speculation as to whether an umbrella, held correctly, might actually help her run by taking some of her weight, and glanced towards the man jogging so effortlessly by her side.

'We're talking Easter Egg Hunt?'

'Of course,' he said briskly, his feet never skipping a beat. 'Isn't that why we're here?'

'No, that's not why we're here! I can think of a hundred places where I'd find it easier to discuss this,' she told him.

The smile flicked towards her again.

'Well, as we are here, and as we're slowing down so you can breathe and talk at the same time, what do you think?'

About his smile? Or breathing and talking at the same time?

'I need more information,' she said, using the old ploy of students when faced with a tricky question.

'Well, I haven't developed it much further than that yet,' William grumbled. 'I thought I'd be the ideas person and you could be the practical one and say whether or not they're feasible.'

'You mean you'll have all the fun and I'll do all the work?'

Again the smile flicked towards her.

'I'm a manager from way back. Comes with the territory, I suppose. Teaching is largely about organising other people, telling them where to look something up, how to find out what they need to know, making them explore the subject for themselves rather than be spoonfed information they regurgitate for an examination then conveniently forget.'

'But we all forget a lot of what we learn for exams,' Prue protested.

He gave a funny little bow.

'My point precisely—but you know where to look it up when you need that information again, don't you?'

She did the head-shaking thing again, wondering if it would ever be possible to keep up with the workings of his mind—or win an argument with him!

Not that it would matter when he'd be gone in a month.

'You look tired. Have I pushed you too far? Too soon? Too fast?'

He'd stopped and had taken hold of her arm. Had he been watching her so closely he'd caught a glimpse of the sudden sadness that had swept over her at the thought of his departure from her life?

'I'm not that tired,' she told him, gently removing her arm from his grasp as the warmth radiated through her yet again. 'But we might walk back.' She smiled up into brown eyes softened by concern. 'Briskly, of course.'

Which was how she treated her wayward thoughts, pulling them briskly into line. She barely knew the man so why should she be fretting over his eventual departure? No being sidetracked from her studies, no emotional overload, no *men*! Remember!

'I'll think about the ward-by-ward idea this afternoon,' she promised, mainly to ease the guilt she felt as she mentally reduced him to an incidental and very temporary episode in her existence.

'I knew you would,' he replied, and she instantly regretted her concession. The damn man was too used by half to getting his own way!

'So, I'll see you at nine,' he said as they made their way

through the high-vaulted glass entrance to the hospital. 'Thanks for keeping me company on the run.'

It was an offhand remark but something in the way he said it stopped her forward momentum.

'I-I thought this exercise was for my benefit, not yours,' she stuttered.

His smile lurked around his lips for a moment, then disappeared as he went for plaintive again.

'But that doesn't mean I can't enjoy it, does it?'

I will not shake my head, Prue told herself firmly. She settled on a sardonic look instead, and walked away from him.

Staying away from him was harder. He'd not only turned up on Tuesday evening, right on time, and stayed for several hours discussing everything under the sun, and resolving nothing about the Easter Egg Hunt, but he seemed to haunt her at the hospital, appearing like a genie from a bottle in the most unexpected places.

'Do you have a copy of my work schedule and follow me around?' she asked on Thursday as they ran companionably, and still slowly, through the park.

'Do you know,' he answered, swerving around a slim blonde pedestrian and avoiding the dog attached to her by a lead, 'I was going to ask you the same question. Barely an hour goes past that I don't trip over you somewhere in the hospital.'

By now she had enough control over her neck muscles not to shake her head at every other statement he made. In fact, his remarks challenged her, and she was beginning to enjoy the verbal battles between them.

'I didn't think you'd notice,' she retorted. 'Among the flock of female staff who positively hang on every word you utter, I'd only be part of the crowd.'

'Ah, but a dissenting voice is always noticed,' he reminded her. '*You* certainly don't hang on every word I utter. In fact, you've a distressing tendency to argue.'

'You're far too used to getting your own way,' she told him. 'It must come from being top dog in your own particular pond.'

'Fish,' he corrected. 'Top fish if we're talking ponds. You're mixing your metaphors.'

She chuckled at the thought of William with fins and a tail, then stopped when she realised she no longer had a companion. He was a few paces back, and behaving in a most peculiar manner, peering suspiciously around like an amateur spy afraid of being followed.

She walked back.

'Something wrong?'

'It's the damn bells again,' he muttered at her. 'I can't believe it. One chance remark by Isobel and now I'm hearing bells. Tell me you can hear them,' he pleaded.

Prue listened, then smiled and pointed to a side path up ahead of them.

'Hare Krishnas,' she said. 'The people who wear yellow robes. They go for little bells and often tinkle. You're hearing them, not going mad.'

He sighed his relief, but continued to look at her for a moment—intently—as if she might be harbouring bells somewhere on her person.

'Why do they worry you so much?' she asked as they fell into their rhythm again. 'I mean, I hear bells and assume someone somewhere is ringing them. I don't get all hot and bothered over who or where.'

He glanced her way, then turned back and concentrated on the path ahead.

Didn't answer.

Should she try again? Ask where Isobel, whom he'd mentioned in conjunction with the bells, came into it?

She decided against that idea. Perhaps he *was* suffering

from the loss of his fiancée, and the bells were a reminder of the wedding he didn't have.

He was a complex man—a brilliant man—but no doubt he was still human enough to feel pain. She suspected his way of dealing with it would be to intellectualise it, and, if that didn't work, banish it to the furthest corner of his mind.

Where it resurfaced when he heard bells?

She sighed, wishing she'd taken more notice of her psychology lectures.

'You're getting tired? I don't want you overdoing things. We'll walk from here.'

It took Prue a moment to work out what he was saying, then she looked around at their surroundings. They were still at what she considered the outward part of their circuit, not yet up to the faster pace that preceded the slower return.

'I'm not tired,' she told him, and moved faster to prove her point.

'Well, that's the fourth time you've sighed, so, if you're not tired, what are you worrying about? The Easter thing? I'm free tonight. I thought we might eat together again and talk about it over dinner. Jill Philp, one of the teachers, suggested we use the closed-circuit hospital television and I thought, instead of us beating our brains out thinking of clues, we could get the patients to do it. Make that the ward-by-ward effort and guessing the answers an individual thing.'

Once again Prue had some mental adjusting to do. Unfortunately she found it difficult to switch from concern over William's psyche and possible hidden suffering to Easter eggs quickly enough to think of an excuse to get out of eating with him.

'What did you do with your evenings before you landed at Lizzie's and got stuck with Mark's twin projects and getting me fit?' she demanded after she'd weakly agreed that pasta sounded tempting, and, yes, Latino's did serve tasty food at the right price.

He looked puzzled.

'I probably go to meetings,' he finally suggested. 'Being out of the university environment must be giving me the extra free time. My secretary doesn't pass on any but the most essential of messages, but, believe me, within the academic world one could spend one's entire life at meetings. Those who organise them insist it's all to do with consensus and reasoned debate, but I've often felt most organisations, particularly one as diverse as a university, could benefit from a benevolent dictatorship.'

Prue smiled.

'The hospital certainly runs better under that system,' she agreed. 'The management team have skills the medical staff could never equal. They're the people who keep the whole place running, leaving the doctors, therapists and nurses free to do what they're trained to do.'

They were walking now, and once again she was able to absorb the beauty of her surroundings. It seeped into her soul, warming her from within, making her feel more aware, more alive, than she had for ages.

'What's on for you this afternoon?' William asked.

Once again, she had to shift her mental gears.

'Patient appointments with Mark. Actually, you might be in on at least one of them. Mr and Mrs Wells are bringing Marcie in at four.'

The beauty of the park at lunch-time faded slightly as she thought ahead to what was sure to be a sticky situation.

'Don't worry,' William said, touching her lightly on the arm. 'I *will* be there.'

The touch was *worse* than a cattle prod! Not that she'd ever actually been prodded by one; it just felt worse. Electric currents racing along her nerves and making her stomach feel jittery.

'Did I look worried?' she demanded, hiding her reaction under brusqueness.

He smiled, and the cattle-prod effect was magnified as he lifted his hand from her arm and stroked one finger gently down between her eyebrows.

'You get just one tiny and very faint wrinkle there when you begin to frown, and your eyes lose their sparkle.'

Eyes lose their sparkle? What kind of answer was that?

She stepped away from him for his eyes were smiling into hers, and his mouth was far too close.

Far too tempting.

No men, remember.

No distractions!

'I think the Leskis are coming in as well,' she said, hoping the switch from personal to professional would reinforce her thoughts. 'The little boy who was admitted the day Penny went home.'

She felt a wash of sadness, for Penny had died the following day.

'I called in to see Caroline and Justin last night.'

Once again William surprised her with the breadth of his activities.

'They're both feeling stricken, but in a way relieved the worst is over. Now they can get on with their grieving.'

They walked in silence back towards the hospital. Prue was glad when they could separate, she heading off to the doctors' mess to change, he to wherever he had hung his three-piece suit, then on to whatever lunch appointment he had.

'I'll catch up with you later,' he said, touching her lightly on the shoulder as if he'd guessed she was trying to distance herself.

She nodded in response and hurried away. Why were all her reactions to this man so exaggerated? The sympathy she'd felt for him when he'd talked of bells and Isobel—

was it the woman's name that was linked to bells in his subconscious?—had been like a fist grasping and squeezing at her heart.

Yet when he'd touched her forehead, that same organ had fluttered in her chest like a trapped bird against imprisoning bars.

And then there were the daffodils. They came up every year, without fail, some time in late winter or early spring. So why were they especially golden when she ran with William through the park?

She checked her vital signs. No, she wasn't feverish, pulse—now they'd gone their separate ways—quite steady. PMT? Wrong time of the month for that excuse, not that she was aware of ever having suffered it.

She hurried on, as if speed might help her escape her thoughts, changed and presented herself back downstairs, ready for the afternoon appointments.

'You're three quarters of an hour early,' Claire told her. 'Are you skipping lunch? That's silly, especially when you're exercising. Off you go to the canteen and have a salad or something light.'

Prue stared at her, unable to believe she'd completely forgotten about lunch.

'I really must pull myself together!' she said to Claire, then she charged out the door, not wanting to explain.

The Leskis were the first appointment and, well fed, Prue greeted them when the nurse seconded from Outpatients for these appointments showed them in.

'Jill will weigh and measure Michael, and check his general health,' she explained to the parents. 'It's easier if he and you stay here in this room, and we send the other specialists to you. The dietitian will be first. There's no special diet for children with arthritis but children suffering various forms of the disease are often poor eaters. They need to be tempted to eat and the dietitian will give you ideas of how to boost the nutritional value of what they do eat.'

'I've a pretty good idea about that kind of thing,' Brian Leski said. 'Ideas like adding cheese or eggs to gravies, extra milk powder to sweets or sauces. Michael is a picky eater, but it's up to us to make sure that what he does eat is good for him.'

Prue smiled at the earnest man who held his little boy so tenderly on his lap. She had no doubt he gave freely of his love to all his children, and her admiration for him was tinged with envy.

'Then the various therapists will pop in. William Alexander is doing a locum for our usual physiotherapist, but he will talk to you about exercises. The basis of the exercise is to encourage Michael to live as normal a life as possible, so most of it is play-based. Crystal, our occupational therapist, will advise on toys, suggest objects most households have that might help Michael move about more easily.'

'Will we have to buy much? Brian wondered about a walker.' It was Maureen who questioned her this time.

'Ask William and Crystal that question, but, at a guess, I'd say no. Michael is reluctant to walk because standing on his leg is painful, but if he doesn't use it the joint could contract. Hopefully, medication will ease the pain, but stiffness will remain.'

'So he needs to be weight-bearing?' Brian suggested, and Prue nodded.

'As much as possible. Put his toys on a low table—a coffee-table would be ideal. Encourage him to stand and play with them. Your other children might play games with him, hiding his toys under cushions on furniture so he has to pull himself up to search for them.'

'The kids would love that,' Maureen said. 'Talk about a bunch of teases!'

'They'll help keep him on his feet,' Brian agreed. 'Once we know it's okay for him to be moving about, and explain it to the older ones, they'll see it happens.'

Prue had a fearful vision of Michael toppling over from exhaustion.

'Check with William how much is too much,' she warned the enthusiastic parents. 'And remember normal! That's what we're after.'

'Do we see Dr Gregory today?' Maureen asked.

Prue smiled at the hesitation in her voice. Brian might be at home in this environment, but, like many parents, Maureen was a little over-awed.

'He's at the end of the line,' Prue told her. 'Once Michael's been put through the hoops here, Jill will show you into his room and he'll go over the results of the tests, X-rays and scans with you.'

'It's a good service,' Brian said.

'The best,' Prue agreed. 'Or so we like to think, although I suppose most speciality units run on much the same lines. We're actually based on an American model because the founder studied in the United States. That explains why we still use the JRA initials which stand for Juvenile Rheumatoid Arthritis as often as we use JCA—for Juvenile Chronic Arthritis—which is a more common term over here.'

'Actually, JCA is more correct,' Brian pointed out, 'as it isn't rheumatism, is it?'

Prue smiled at him.

'You'll keep us on our toes,' she told him. 'Rheumatism is a term used for pain and stiffness in the joints, so, yes, it can be called rheumatism. Did you know the word derives from the Greek, *rheuma*, which means a stream and was used to describe the pain suffered by people who worked in damp cold places—by a stream, for instance?'

'I'd rather the rheumatoid word in there than chronic,' Maureen said. 'Chronic always sounds so bad—so final.'

'Well, whatever you call it, it isn't final in the sense that Michael will probably outgrow it. What we hope to do in the meantime is keep his joints free from damage so he doesn't carry long-term effects of the disease into adulthood.'

She was interrupted by the arrival of the dietitian, and she left the parents and patient, moving on to the next appointment, again doing the explanations and preliminaries before the patient moved on to see Mark.

By four o'clock when the Wells family arrived, Mark was only twenty minutes behind schedule. Prue heard Claire apologising for the delay, then a loud voice complaining.

'Trouble ahead!' she muttered to herself, shuffling one patient and his smiling mother out of Mark's office and another, plus family support, in.

Sensing she'd be more use in the waiting room, she made her way to where the protests were growing more voluble.

'Ah, at last someone with some authority here,' Mr Wells said loudly. He looked her up and down, then added, 'Well, I'm assuming you have authority. I'm Jeff Wells and this is my wife Kirsten. We're both busy people, and coming along here today was very inconvenient. Although I don't know why we should have been called in when Dr Gregory knows our nanny has authority to deal with any problem concerning Marcie.'

'Dr Gregory will explain,' Prue said in what she hoped was a soothing voice, although she was so angry at his attitude she was sure he could hear the bite behind her words. 'Unfortunately, things don't always run to time in a hospital. But no doubt you know that in your own professional lives. Are your appointments always on time?'

Mrs Wells' smile was apologetic but she didn't introduce herself, merely nodding acknowledgment of Prue's direct hit. She was sitting down, holding Marcie on her knee, her hands clutching the little girl's waist as if uncertain of her balance.

'We don't make a habit of it,' Jeff Wells blustered, too arrogant to back down.

Prue would have retorted, 'Nor do we,' but something about the child's position—the tentativeness of her mother—had opened floodgates deep within her, freeing dark sadness that surged and washed, like storm-tossed seas, throughout her body.

'Will you excuse me?' she said, and blundered towards the door of the waiting room, needing to escape, to catch her breath and find the strength to slam those floodgates shut again.

How could they surface—just like that—when she thought them gone for ever?

She was biting back an involuntary cry of pain when strong hands gripped her shoulders and she was held against a broad, but unfamiliar chest.

Not that it stayed unfamiliar for long! Her senses, activated by the warmth, told her it was William.

'Are you okay?' he asked anxiously. 'Damn it all, woman, I knew you looked tired when we ran. You should have said. Told me you weren't up to it. You're as white as a sheet. Is it a headache? Stomach upset? Summer flu?'

She couldn't answer, although the warmth, plus the solidity of his body, the strength of the fingers biting into her flesh, all combined to turn back the tide and shove the past back where it belonged.

'I'm okay,' she mumbled against his waistcoat. 'I was silly enough to let Mr Wells get to me.'

William shook her gently.

'Foolish woman!' he said, his voice softly chiding. 'I thought I was going to deal with Mr and Mrs Wells.'

Prue, realising she was making a public spectacle of herself with her face buried in William's chest in the corridor leading from Outpatients, pushed away.

'Mine was no more than a preliminary skirmish,' she explained, hoping she sounded more together than she felt. Although the past had receded, now the present was causing turmoil, the feel of William's body seemingly imprinted on her skin. 'Mark's running slightly late and Mr Wells is not a man who likes being kept waiting.'

'I'll see to Mr Wells,' William assured her, then, apparently oblivious of the public situation, he put his arm around her shoulders and ushered her back into the suite of rooms that housed the unit.

'Do you want a coffee to calm your nerves or would you prefer to watch an expert at work?' he whispered to Prue, dropping his arm but remaining close to her.

She dredged up a smile although she feared facing the Wells family again in a hundred years would be too soon.

'I guess I'd better stick with you,' she said. 'After all, we're going to have to show a united front in this situation.'

William smiled at her, and the now-familiar excitement skittered along her nerves. She'd given up telling them it was only a smile, and now found herself enjoying the charge!

If nothing else, it made her feel alive!

'Mr Wells? Mrs Wells? I'm William Alexander.'

William dropped to a crouch so he was level with Marcie.

'Hi, Marcie, how are you today? What's this? Not a rabbit hiding behind your pigtail?'

Prue, who hadn't seen him produce the tiny fluffy toy, was as surprised and delighted as Marcie.

'We only allow her fully washable toys.' Jeff Wells put his dampener on the moment, but William rolled with the punch.

'I bought it at Foams, which only stocks the best quality, washable toys,' he assured the man.

He stood up as he answered, leaving the rabbit tucked into Marcie's hands, her little fingers already exploring the long pink ears.

And although Prue was willing to swear he wasn't standing straighter, he somehow looked taller—more impressive.

Perhaps it was the suit.

'I'm filling in for Annette, the physiotherapist, and I'm actually the person who asked for this appointment,' William explained, while Prue hauled her mind off admiration for men in suits—well, one man in a suit—and concentrated on what was happening. 'Mark will explain our concerns but I'd like to do some hands-on work with the two of you so maybe while you're waiting...'

He left the suggestion up in the air and it was Mrs Wells who jumped in.

'Are you talking about Marcie's exercises? We really don't know anything about those. Inga does them.'

'I told you we should have sent her along. It was you who decided to pander to the hospital and insisted we both come.' Jeff Wells spoke so angrily Prue waited for his wife to retaliate, but she seemed unperturbed. Perhaps that was how he always spoke to her.

'You were asked to attend this one appointment because we felt it was more appropriate to express our concerns to both of you. After all, as Marcie's parents, responsibility for her welfare rests with you.'

'Are you saying Inga's incompetent? Is that what you're getting at? She's from the best agency, highly recommended, and she loves Marcie and understands her condition.'

Jeff was blustering again, but Mrs Wells had caught the drift of the conversation and was looking worried.

'You said welfare,' she said to William. 'Do you think Inga's ill-treating her?'

Her hands tightened on her daughter's waist, then she folded the little girl against her body and gave her a cuddle.

Claire appeared at that moment, and signalled for them all to go into Mark's office.

'No,' William replied quietly to Mrs Wells as he offered his hand to help her to her feet. 'Not deliberately. Come on, Dr Gregory will explain.'

Unfortunately, Mark's explanations only made Jeff Wells angrier, his face showing an unbecoming flush of rage as he tried to argue that the unit was overreacting.

'I can see what you mean,' Mrs Wells said. She'd sat down again with Marcie, and had been examining her limbs. 'I *can* see faint bruises.'

'Well, it's all your fault,' her husband stormed. 'If you'd been content to stay at home with the child like a normal mother instead of pushing this nonsense of carrying on with your career—'

Prue felt nausea rise to her throat as echoes of similar words rang like William's haunting bells in her head. But the man's put-down, and her reaction to it, brought anger in its wake. She turned expectantly to Mrs Wells. Surely now she'd fight back, stand up for herself?

The woman's hands were trembling, and Prue, realising just how distraught she was, got up from her chair and went to her.

'Can I get you something?' she asked. 'Take Marcie for a while? We realise this must be a terrible shock, but we'd have been negligent in our duty of care to a patient to let it go unmentioned.'

Mrs Wells' blue eyes gazed piteously into hers.

'He said he wanted me to continue working,' she whispered. 'He said we needed two incomes to maintain a decent lifestyle. I love my work. I'm good at it. He suggested a nanny, found Inga and everything. I thought it was the one thing on which we did agree.'

Prue closed her eyes against the woman's pain, then opened them and patted her gently on the shoulder. She didn't take Marcie, realising Mrs Wells needed something solid to cling to right now, even if it was only a small child.

'Recriminations won't solve anything,' Mark said, bringing the meeting back to order with quiet common sense. 'What does need to be done is for us to show the two of you Marcie's exercise programme, then for you to either do it each day, or supervise Inga doing it, until you're certain she's not pushing Marcie too hard.'

'As I said earlier, we don't think it's deliberate cruelty,' William added. 'More over-enthusiasm to do the right thing by the child. Although she must have been aware of the bruises, so perhaps she was under the impression this was normal. It's easy for medical people to assume people understand what we are telling them, and with a language barrier thrown in...'

As William let his defence of Inga trail into nothingness, Jeff Wells straightened.

'Well, language barrier or not, she'll have to go!' he said, and Prue, who'd been kneeling by Mrs Wells and Marcie, found herself shooting upright.

'That would be disastrous,' she said. 'At this stage of her illness, Marcie needs normality, routine, people she's learned to love and trust around her. She needs stability, not a new nanny.'

'The decisions we make for our child's welfare are not your concern, Doctor,' Jeff Wells said coldly. Then he turned to William. 'I suggest you show us these all-important exercises and let us get out of here. It's already past Marcie's teatime, so how's that for breaking her routine?'

William again offered his hand to Mrs Wells, then, without a word, led the family out of Mark's office. As the door shut behind him, Prue dropped her head into her hands.

'Well, that was a disaster,' Mark said, so cheerfully Prue looked up at him.

He was smiling!

'I don't see how you can take it so lightly. Or why you're not carpeting me for unprofessional behaviour. I'm sorry. I shouldn't have let him get under my skin.'

'He was getting under everyone's skin, Prue,' Mark said gently. 'And it does us all good to say what we think sometimes, although why that woman stays with him, I can't imagine. A more pompous, self-important, arrogant bore I have yet to meet.'

'And a bully,' Prue added. 'I kept hoping she'd stand up to him, then worrying about Marcie being present while we discussed her and Inga.'

'I certainly wouldn't have had the child in the room if I'd guessed how he'd react,' Mark agreed. 'The reason she was included was so they'd see what we were talking about. If they were so remiss as not to notice it themselves, then telling them about it was unlikely to convince them. We had to show them the injuries.'

He leaned over to his intercom and pressed a button.

'Think you could rustle up some coffee?' he asked Claire over the intercom. 'You've a couple of shell-shocked doctors in here.'

They were sipping at their coffee and discussing another patient when William returned.

'Well, that went well, didn't it?' he said cheerfully, but his eyes, when he looked at Prue, were filled with concern.

'I want to do a ward round before I finish up so I'll leave you to fill Mark in on the therapy session,' she said, leaving the room without looking at him.

CHAPTER EIGHT

WILLIAM turned to Mark and raised his eyebrows, but Mark had apparently missed his junior's distress.

'Will they do the therapy themselves?' Mark asked. 'Or would we have been better off spending time with Inga, showing her what was required?'

'In retrospect, it might have been the way to go,' William admitted, 'but I still believe it's the parents' responsibility.' He hesitated, then added, 'And maybe we've triggered something that needed to be thrashed out between the pair of them.'

'Or divorce proceedings,' Mark said gloomily. Then he seemed to shrug off his dour mood. 'Let's talk about something else. I've given Prue the replies from the GPs we surveyed, but the Easter business should probably take precedence at the moment. Can I tell the powers-that-be it's under control?'

William closed his eyes for a moment. Prue was right—he was a congenital volunteer, taking on far more than he could handle.

'Yes.' He told the lie with such conviction he almost believed it himself. The way Prue had looked earlier this afternoon, Easter festivities had been the last thing on her mind.

'Good man!' Mark said. 'Now, about this theory of deep muscles in the back and joints—'

The discussion took them through until Claire popped her head into the office to tell Mark she was going home and as it was already after six, he should consider doing the same.

'All right for these single chaps like the Prof to be here all hours, but Anna's probably looking to you to give her a hand with the preparations for Saturday night.'

Mark looked stricken.

'Good heavens, Claire, why didn't you remind me? I had a list of things I was supposed to pick up for her.'

'I'll let you go,' William told him, but as Mark and Claire both departed, and the therapists' office was also deserted, he felt a sudden surge of loneliness. As if everyone but him had someone waiting for them, somewhere.

The sensation was so new, not to say unexpected, he rationalised it by telling himself he was out of his usual environment, although, deep down, he suspected he'd feel equally unsettled if he were alone in his office at the university right now.

He scratched through the papers that were apparently breeding on his temporary desk and found the number he needed to bleep Prue. After all, they'd made arrangements to eat together but hadn't settled on a time.

She phoned almost immediately.

'I'm leaving now,' she told him, when he asked about her immediate plans.

'So am I,' he said. 'If you're not pulling some horrendously early shift in the morning, why don't you leave your car here and let me drive you home? We can grab a bite to eat on the way, have a talk, and I'll call by your place to drive you back to work in the morning.'

Silence echoed down the phone.

'Are you still there?' he demanded, something that felt very like anxiety coiling in his stomach.

'Yes!'

'Yes, what?' he asked grumpily, because anxious stomachs always made him grumpy. 'Yes, you're still there, or yes to my idea? I'm offering a simple common-sense suggestion, not asking you to join me on an attack on the Tower of London, you know.'

'I was trying to remember if I'm on call tonight. Not first call, but second or third. I probably am and should have my car at home.'

'Then we'll take your car,' he said. 'But let's get out of this place. I've had enough of it for one day, and I suspect you feel the same way.'

Another silence, during which time he decided the stomach problem might be hunger.

'I'll meet you at the unit in a few minutes,' she said, and the hunger went away.

She was smiling so brightly when she appeared, he decided he must have imagined her earlier distress.

'I've had an idea,' she told him, positively glowing with delight. The excitement in her eyes started more turmoil in his stomach.

And various other parts of his body.

'So tell,' he prompted, and her smile grew even wider as she threw her arms wide.

She gave a preliminary, 'Ta-dah!' of a trumpet call, and announced, 'The rabbit who lost his eggs!'

She was so obviously pleased with herself he knew it must mean something. But what? Was his brain as affected by hunger as his stomach?

'Explain more to the professor who's lost his marbles!' he begged, and she chuckled.

He listened automatically for bells and was relieved when none rang, although he thought he could hear someone whistling somewhere. And the non-ringing of bells wasn't helping him understand about the rabbit.

'We have a rabbit, you see,' she said, all but dancing in her excitement. 'Not a real rabbit, of course, but we hire a rabbit suit and, providing it's a good size, different staff members can be inside it, depending on who has the time.

First of all, as soon as possible, the rabbit goes around the wards, telling all the children he's lost his eggs—'

Light dawned. In fact it positively flooded into his bemused brain.

'And they think up clues for him to follow looking for them! You're a genius! It's a great idea.'

He seized her by the waist and swung her around, then gave her a good hug.

Actually, it started out as a hug, but when he realised how neatly her body fitted against his...

'We can include the little ones, because when the rabbit's looking, they can call out hot or cold,' Prue continued.

It took him a moment to assimilate that bit. He'd been getting hot and cold himself, more hot than cold, but shivery at the same time, until she pulled away, looking up into his face to explain this added benefit to her scheme.

'So each ward will have eggs?'

'No. I thought he'd have to find a clue to send him on to somewhere else. If we follow your suggestion of using the TV, we could have patient ''reporters'' following his progress.'

William smiled at her enthusiasm, then was surprised to see the sparkle fade from her eyes, leaving wariness in its wake.

'Well, we'd better be going,' she said briskly. 'I've a notebook in the car. We'll work out the details while we're eating, and I'll jot down what we have to do to get it under way.'

He felt as if he'd been cast adrift and wondered, as he followed her to her car, what had caused the mood change.

Women! Could men ever presume to understand them?

'That's it,' she said, waving to a small, but new model, sedan and using a gizmo to unlock the car doors.

'Very smart,' he said, wondering what she'd think of his ancient but beloved Jag.

Her smile returned, and he sensed she was pleased with his remark.

'I treated myself to it when I began work with Mark,' she said. 'The credit company owns all but the front bumper bar, but I think of it as mine.'

He was surprised by her admission. For some reason, he'd seen her background as well-to-do; imagined she'd come from a family who'd have considered a car the only possible graduation present.

He climbed in, pleased to find the leg room more adequate than he'd imagined.

'We won't be able to park anywhere near the restaurants,' she warned him, driving swiftly but competently out of the car park. 'How far is your place from mine? I've a resident's permit for my square, so if I can find a space, are you happy to walk?'

He was, but something she'd said earlier collided with the sentence.

'You don't have a designated space outside your building?'

She glanced towards him, then, as the traffic lights turned green, concentrated on weaving through the traffic before replying.

'No, but I can usually find somewhere nearby.'

He found himself going hot and cold again.

'So, if you're called out, say at two in the morning, you have to walk to your car.'

Another glance, this time accompanied by a frown.

'It's a very quiet residential area. There aren't many drug deals going down in the leafy environs of Brandon Gardens.'

'You never know!' he muttered, wondering why the thought of her being out on her own in the early hours of the morning should bother him so much.

He slumped back in his seat, folded his arms across his chest, and tried not to think about it.

'There! Right in front! I won't have to dodge the drug dealers if I'm called out tonight!' she said triumphantly, expertly backing the little car into what had looked to him to be too small a space.

'It's no laughing matter,' he told her, put out by her disregard for his concern. 'I'm all in favour of independent women—my mother is one—but safety issues shouldn't be ignored.'

Prue turned to him, smiled, then reached behind her for the large handbag she'd dumped into the back seat.

'See this?' she said, producing a small fat cylinder from her handbag. 'I carry it in my hand when I go out to my car late at night, and when I walk through the hospital car park as well. One press on the button and the thing shrieks so loudly, only the most desperate of muggers wouldn't run for his life.'

William felt both relieved and chastened, but the relief, for some reason, was stronger, and he smiled at her.

She should have bought a bigger car, Prue realised, as the interior shrank so rapidly she could almost taste William's presence, his closeness, in the air. Back when she'd first joined the unit and talked of buying a new vehicle, Crystal and Annette had both told her to go for the bigger model. They'd laughingly joked about her chauffeuring kids around in it before long and she hadn't known them well enough to tell them that wasn't likely.

Now it was far too small, she realised, as she tried to thrust her personal alarm back into her handbag and ended up emptying the whole damn thing on the floor.

'I'd heard about the things women carried in their handbags,' William murmured in awestruck tones, 'but never believed it.'

He reached over to help, retrieving—inevitably, Prue supposed—a pair of lacy knickers.

'I like to have clean underwear if I take a shower at work,' she said, snatching the offending garment from his fingers. 'Didn't Isobel carry a handbag, that the contents of mine should be so fascinating?'

She slapped his hand away from a slim leather wallet that held the only photo she had of her father. She'd rescued it from her mother's murderous destruction of every reminder of him, and tucked it under her mattress because, even at four, the child she'd been had sensed she might one day want it.

'Isobel always had very small receptacles. Large enough for a tube of lipstick and a lace-edged handkerchief, I presumed. Like the Queen, Isobel didn't carry money.'

'Didn't carry money?' Prue echoed, diverted from her task by such a bizarre statement.

'Well, not when she was with me. I told you I'm an old-fashioned man.'

'Antediluvian, don't you mean?' she teased, and was rewarded by a smile of singular sweetness.

Which reminded her of the smallness of her car, the dangerous implications of being so close to William Alexander, and the fact that their relationship, if such it could be called, was purely business.

She shoved the remaining items of junk back into her handbag, promised herself she'd clean it out on her next days off, and opened the car door. She was halfway up the steps to the front door before she remembered she wasn't going home. They were going to eat.

'Do you want to drop something off? Have a wash? Change?' William asked her, and she wondered if her flat, too, would shrink if she invited him in.

Had it on Tuesday when he'd been there?

She couldn't remember. Couldn't think.

Better not to risk it.

'No. Put it down to automatic reaction. Get out of the car and go inside,' she said, hoping her deliberately light tone would seem normal to him.

'Shouldn't automatic reaction include locking your car?' he asked, and her head forgot she'd decided not to shake it any more, and moved from side to side as she tried to comprehend the confusion this man could so effortlessly generate in her mind.

'Automatic automatic,' she said, pressing the remote to lock the doors. Perhaps he'd think she didn't ever do it until she was on her way up the steps.

She walked back down and joined him on the pavement. 'Okay, let's go.'

The smile broke out again and she turned away, walking towards the corner with brisk, determined steps.

To be this affected by a smile was lunacy.

'In a hurry to get down to business, or to get it over and done with so you can get rid of me?' he asked, falling into step beside her and tucking her hand into the crook of his arm.

She glanced towards the man who strode beside her, seeing him in profile and wondering how someone's face could become so familiar after only a few days.

'Not going to answer?' he said, turning in time to catch her watching him.

'Answer what?' she asked blankly, unable to remember any recent conversation.

He chuckled and she felt the sound as well as hearing it as his chest moved beneath his jacket.

'Never mind. We'll talk of more practical things,' he said. 'Do I know the poor blighter you've got lined up for the Easter Bunny part? Or are you going to audition. Must be able to hop. That would be the only prerequisite, surely?'

Prue turned towards him.

'I thought *you'd* volunteer,' she said. 'Don't tell me you're going to go against your nature!'

William looked down at her, the tiny wrinkles gathering at the corners of his eyes as he battled a smile.

'I would, but I'm far too busy,' he said mildly, the smile now tugging at his lips.

'Me too,' Prue agreed, grinning at his nonsense, and with the pleasure she was feeling, walking down an ordinary street with this not-so-ordinary man.

Once again, they chose an outside table, marvelling at how the weather had remained fine, and they *did* talk about the Easter Egg Hunt, although topics of conversation ranged far and wide, well beyond the reason for their eating together.

'So, did you make notes?' William asked, when he became aware of the persistently hovering waiter, and realised they'd overstayed their welcome. He folded a couple of notes inside the bill and passed it to the young man.

'About your boyhood Scout camps? My longing to be a ballerina? The price of hash in bygone days in Turkey?'

He tried to look affronted.

'About the Easter Egg Hunt,' he told her. 'You know Mark expects us to be handling this.'

She smiled at him, and he decided he liked the way the left side of her mouth tilted up just a little more than the right, pressing an almost dimple into her left cheek.

'Yes, I took notes—you saw me writing things down. I'll talk to the teachers about getting some of the older children to make up clues. I think you're right about them rhyming. Much more fun that way. But don't expect them to come up with an unlimited number. It was your idea so you think up some as well, and, no, rude limericks will not be accepted.'

She chuckled and he knew she was remembering the 'juice in the sluice' rhyme he'd made up as an example.

'We should ring a bell,' the waiter said, returning to their table with William's change on a saucer. 'The way they do in some pubs to indicate last drinks.'

Thank heavens you didn't, William thought, but just then the lights flashed on and off. It was a further indication the business was about to close.

Nothing to do with Prue's chuckle!

They walked back towards her place in a companionable silence, her hand tucked into his arm, her body soft and warm against his. She was a very restful companion, he decided. Then remembered her fiery reaction to Mr Wells.

Her apparent distress.

'Why did Marcie's parents bother you so much?'

The softness stiffened, and she edged away from him.

'I don't like parental arguments, especially not when they're carried on in front of children.'

She withdrew her hand to fumble in her handbag, but he guessed it was an excuse to move further from his side. To detach herself emotionally as well as physically. A sure sign she didn't like this conversation.

He didn't push the matter, although his feeling of disappointment that she wouldn't confide in him was disproportionate.

The silence accompanying them now was strained, to say the least, and in the end it was Prue who broke it. Unable to bear the dark cloud of memory that mocked and taunted her, destroying the memories of their meal together and souring the special ambience of their stroll back to her flat.

'You know what they say about people drowning. Their life flashes before their eyes.' She stopped walking and turned to face him, saw the shadow patterns of the budding twigs on the plane tree that the lamplight threw across his face.

'I was drowning in there. My life flashing before my eyes. My parents both worked. My mother claimed it was a joint decision, the need for two incomes for a lifestyle neither had the time to enjoy. I had a nanny—an au pair, actually. A Swedish girl called Brita, whom I adored.'

She paused, then said, 'She went away when I was four. I was devastated. I went to nursery school after that, then boarding-school. Very ordinary childhood in many ways. It was the argument, and the talk of sacking Inga. I'd heard it all before and knew how the disruption could affect Marcie, and at a time when she doesn't need emotional stress.'

Even in the dull light, Prue could read the understanding in William's warm brown eyes. She turned away from it and walked on, wanting not sympathy but closure. A memory eraser that would wipe away the childhood pain and leave her free of its disturbing and persistent influence.

He caught up with her, moved into step beside her, but didn't take her hand again and tuck it in his arm.

'It must be difficult for couples who both want to work to make secure child-care arrangements,' he said, 'although I know plenty who seem to manage.'

Prue knew he was trying to regain the ease they'd had between them, and played along.

'So do I,' she admitted, adding lightly, 'I'm just a little hung up over it.'

There was a pause, and, in order to avoid him querying that last remark, she changed tack.

'And what had you and Isobel planned in the way of family and making provisions for them?'

It was his turn to stop.

'You know, I doubt we'd ever discussed it.'

He looked so genuinely startled she had to believe him.

'Engaged for a hundred years and you didn't get around to discussing family?'

'It was only eight years,' he said in a reproving tone. 'And, anyway, we wouldn't have needed to discuss it. I can imagine how it would have been. Isobel has never work-worked, if you know what I mean.'

'No, I don't,' Prue told him, rather regretting her introduction of Isobel into the conversation.

'Not had a real job,' he explained, which didn't help at all. Fortunately he enlarged on it as they walked on.

'She'd go in to help friends out from time to time, did something in a public relations office now and then, arranged interviews for a couple of magazine editors, went to Ascot and Wimbledon. She was always very busy.'

'So she'd have stayed home when you had children. Been a hands-on mother!'

William looked shocked.

'Good heavens, no. She'd have had a nanny to look after them. But I imagine even supervising a nanny is time-consuming, and she'd have had more time and energy to do that than a young lawyer battling her way up the ladder would have.'

Now Prue was even sorrier she'd introduced Isobel as the image of William returning home to a beautifully ordered flat, like something out of *Harpers and Queen*, being greeted by an immaculately dressed wife and perfect children, was so vivid it made her stomach ache.

Because he fitted right in there.

Look at them right now! William in his three-piece suit, which she knew had adjusted to a day of therapy programmes without looking one whit the worse for wear, while she was in the daggy skirt and blouse she'd worn to work that morning and probably looked like something the cat had dragged in.

'Thanks for walking back with me,' she said when they reached her building. 'Would you like me to run you home? Then I'll know where to collect you in the morning.'

He glanced around the square.

'No. You might lose this spot. I'll walk, it's only a couple of blocks, and I'll meet you back here tomorrow. What time?'

They settled on eight although she suspected that might be a little earlier than William usually went in, and said their goodnights.

Hers firm, his a little tentative.

Had he expected to be invited in?

Surely not. After all, it was a business relationship, nothing else.

The phone dragged her out of a deep sleep and, as she reached for the receiver, knowing it was a call to go in to work, she realised how stupid the idea of only taking one car home had been.

William's idea—yet she'd fallen in with it.

It was four o'clock and experience told her she wouldn't be leaving the hospital until her day's work was done. And she had no idea how to contact him.

Shelving William—which wasn't easy as she found him intruding into her mental life more and more—she pulled on jeans and a long-sleeved knit shirt in a vivid blue. Experience again. Bright colours made her feel more alert in the early morning.

She grabbed a change of clothes, a slightly more presentable outfit for later in the day, as she had ward rounds with Mark on Fridays, and left the flat.

The hospital, usually quiet at this unseemly hour, was in a frenzy of activity. The discovery of toxic fumes seeping from an ammonia storage facility near a large general hospital had forced the evacuation of all the patients, Lizzie's being called on to take most of the children.

'So it doesn't matter that they've come complete with files, and even their own staff, we still have to go through the motions of clerking them.' Robyn Devlin was on duty in General Medical, and she explained it to Prue above the din of wailing children. 'Not to mention comforting them, and our own patients who aren't used to being moved around in the middle of the night. Do you want a nurse to give you a hand?'

Prue glanced around, and shook her head.

'Any spare hands would be better employed with the comforting side of things,' she suggested. 'I'll work my way through the newcomers. After all, they're not going anywhere. Anywhere special you'd like me to start?'

'There's a three-year-old in the far corner of the ward. He's okay but his mother, who'd stayed in with him, is very distressed. Once he's officially ours, we might be able to settle them both down.'

Prue headed for the far corner of the ward, to a curtained-off cubicle where a rosy-cheeked toddler sat up in a cot, sucking his thumb and watching his weeping mother with an expression of concern in his huge blue eyes.

'He was only in for tests,' the mother cried, when she realised Prue had joined them. 'Something to do with his liver, the doctor said. Why couldn't we go home instead of coming here? How will anyone know where we are? How do I know he didn't get some gas in him?'

Prue guessed she'd reached the real cause of the panic and moved to allay at least that fear.

'From what I can gather, the problem wasn't in the hospital but nearby. He wouldn't have breathed in the gas.'

She lifted the chart from the slot at the foot of the cot and began to read it.

Jamie Tresize wouldn't have been sent home as he was booked for a scan with IV contrast, a dye used to show up better on the computerised radiography equipment. He'd been seen by his local doctor and referred on when he continued to suffer weight loss, accompanied by a low-grade fever.

'He's had more tests than most kids twice his age. Why won't they say what's wrong?'

Mrs Tresize had stopped crying, but Prue knew that was probably because she felt less alone with another adult in the room. Less vulnerable.

She was right about the tests. He'd had all the usual blood tests, and also a lumbar puncture for CSF tests. The specialist had ruled out various nasty complaints that had liver involvement, and now appeared to be investigating a bacterial liver or biliary tract disease.

'It's hard enough having a child in hospital, without being shunted around in the middle of the night,' Prue comforted the woman with her understanding. Then she turned to Jamie and spoke quietly to him, explaining what she was going to do.

'You see,' she said, 'if you suddenly get better, we need to know if it happened here at Lizzie's or if perhaps the ambulance ride did the trick,' she told the little boy as she checked blood pressure, then pulse and temperature.

In actual fact, part of the hospital's duty of care was to know the exact state of each patient when they were officially admitted, and, as no one knew for certain how long they'd have these extra patients, they had to go through the procedures.

'Is he always so biddable?' Prue asked when she'd finished her examination and Jamie had settled back in his cot and, without a murmur of complaint, drifted back to sleep.

'Nearly always!' Mrs Tresize smiled down at her slumbering infant. 'I don't suppose there's anywhere I can get a cuppa? And phone my mum. She was coming in to be with him in the morning so I could go to work. She'll be heading off soon if I don't catch her.'

Prue directed her back to the desk where tea, a telephone

and, no doubt, more sympathy and understanding would be organised.

The next child was asleep, though how anyone could sleep through the racket in the adjacent bed was beyond Prue's understanding. She moved towards the noise-machine, a wailing six-year-old who was fighting the nurse who tried to comfort her.

'If you're here with us for a day or two, you might see our Easter Bunny,' she told the little girl. 'He'll be coming around any day now, counting how many children are in here so he has the right number of eggs.'

The wailing stopped and dark brown eyes peered suspiciously at Prue.

'Chocolate eggs or a sweetie egg?' she demanded.

Prue pretended to consider this while she scanned the child's file.

'I think he'll probably bring both,' she said.

Urinary tract infection. The child had been on—was still on—parenteral ampicillin and aminoglycoside to combat a systemic infection. Urine analysis was being done every forty-eight hours and the last notation from the case doctor suggested the child, if she remained afebrile for the next twelve hours, would be ready to be switched to oral penicillin.

According to Robyn, the doctors from the hospital would be following their patients over here, at least for twenty-four hours while the ducts throughout the hospital were tested for any indication of toxic fumes.

Once again Prue explained the reason why she had to check, and the little girl, Polly, stopped wailing and took an interest in the proceedings.

'At school we were going to make Easter eggs,' she told Prue. 'We were going to use real eggs then wrap them in paper and boil them and they'd be like hard-boiled eggs only all pretty colours. Now I'm going to miss out.'

'Maybe you could do that here,' Prue said, as another idea for the Easter Egg Hunt sparked in her brain. 'I'll find out for you.'

She was fairly certain that neither the nursing staff nor the school staff would fancy the idea of small patients boiling eggs, but surely it could be done if safeguards were put in place. All the wards had the facilities for heating milk and other drinks—so boiling eggs should be a cinch.

She was on the last child—the one who'd been asleep—when she remembered William and wondered how on earth she could get in touch with him. Would his phone number be down in the unit somewhere?

Or should she phone Pat?

And explain why they'd gone home together the previous evening? Start speculation that would delight the unit staff and undoubtedly spread beyond that small enclave?

She could phone Mark.

A quick glance at the clock told her phoning Mark wasn't an option. It was after seven and he'd already be on his way in to work.

Bleep him?

She was considering her options when the cause of her concern walked in, large as life and twice as cheerful.

'Good morning,' he said brightly. 'Sister told me I'd find you somewhere up here.'

Prue was too busy telling herself he was just a colleague to catch all the details of his explanation, but she got the gist of it.

Or thought she had.

Although, when she considered the bits she'd caught, it didn't seem very likely she'd got it right.

She frowned at him.

'You're saying you heard about the fume business on the radio, phoned the hospital to see where patients had been taken, phoned me and when I didn't answer assumed I'd been called in, then you *ran* into work?'

It was the last bit that seemed the most unlikely, but he nodded as if running the however-many miles was nothing.

'Why?' she asked, when it occurred to her she needed more information.

'Because I didn't have a car,' he said patiently. 'We were coming in together, remember?'

Men!

'I don't mean why run, although it seems very excessive to me, but why come in so early? I would have phoned you to explain as soon as I was free here. You're not due at work for ages.'

'Well, now I've seen you,' he explained, 'I'm going up to Chests. There were a couple of CF kids at that hospital. As they're in and out all the time, their parents rarely stay over, so I thought they might welcome a familiar face.'

He walked away and Prue stared after him. He'd come to see her to tell her not to worry about his transport to the hospital, she told herself, not for any other reason.

And not that she should care, either way.

CHAPTER NINE

THE day remained as busy as it had begun, with the stray medical staff more a hindrance than a help as they had to be guided or given directions or have routines explained to them.

'Be nice if all hospitals could run on the same system so we all slotted more easily into each other's way of doing things,' Prue complained to Mark after a particularly snippy young registrar had told her off for some shortcoming in Lizzie's way of doing things.

'It's human nature to imagine our way is always superior,' he reminded her. 'Even if we started off the same, it wouldn't take long before little changes crept in. Besides, the physical surrounds are so different. Even the needs of patients, not to mention staffing structure.'

They were heading back to the unit, running very late for the weekly case meeting but relieved the day was nearly over.

'You're late, you two!'

William's voice from behind brought them both to a halt.

'And you're not?' Mark asked him, while Prue felt her tiredness drain away, replaced by an inner excitement that didn't fizz or bubble but was simply there.

William did his affronted look.

'I've already been, then I came to look for my co-conspirator. I thought if you started asking nasty questions about the Easter business, we should at least tell the same story.'

He turned to Prue and smiled.

'And where were you at lunch-time?' he asked with

mock severity. 'Just because I ran to work, doesn't mean you can miss your exercise.'

'I'll go on ahead and get organised,' Mark broke in. 'And as for Prue, she's been up since the wee hours, so give the girl a break. Running, indeed.'

Prue smiled her thanks at Mark's championship of her.

'I think he's got too much on his plate to worry about Easter,' she said, turning her attention to William. 'And if he does ask, we'll say it's all under control.'

'And is it?' William asked, his dark eyes studying her intently.

'More or less,' she told him, and saw a glint in the darkness, the beginnings of a smile. 'That's where I was at lunch-time, as it happens. Checking out costume hire, one large rabbit suit being delivered Monday, talking to staff and the teachers, trying to get ahead of this thing. I want to get it going.'

'Well, I'll forgive you,' he said magnanimously. 'But just this once. So, shall we go?'

He held out his arm and she slipped her hand in, the response as natural as breathing.

'Are we telling Mark the idea or just that it's organised?' he asked.

She heard pleasure in his voice and grinned, knowing he shared her growing excitement in the simple task of providing some extra pleasure for their young patients.

'Just that it's organised,' she told him. 'Let's keep it as a surprise for everyone.'

The case meeting went longer than expected, due mainly to the need to discuss Marcie Wells and put safeguards in place in case of repercussions from the meeting with her parents.

'They really bother you, don't they?' William said as he accompanied her to the car park when they'd finally finished.

'I shouldn't let them,' she said, but she couldn't deny it so she changed the conversation instead, giving him a list of the wards which would be involved in the Easter Egg Hunt and suggesting he start thinking of rhyming clues to take the rabbit from one to the other.

'Like, "Ring the bell and light the light, Nurse will come to tuck you tight",' he said, and Prue *had* to shake her head.

'Tell me you didn't think that up on the spur of the moment,' she begged. 'Tell me you lay awake all last night working on rhyming couplets.'

He grinned at her, a smile so full of delight, she felt its warmth right down to her toes.

'Don't expect too much on the strength of one example,' he warned. 'The darn thing's been running around in my head since you suggested we might have to come up with some clues. It was like a stray dog—followed me home.'

'So you had to keep it,' Prue agreed. 'Well, it's a start. I assume the clue would be hidden at the nurses' station, near the console that lights up when the kids press their call buttons. Now all you have to do is—how many? Twelve? Thirteen more. I thought we'd start in General Medical where it would be easier for me to get it organised.'

'And the televising side of things? Can you work that?'

Prue nodded.

'Young Nick Jones, a bright thirteen-year-old from Orthopaedics, is going to be the first interviewer, and a mate of his, in a wheelchair from knee surgery, will do the camera work. The pair of them have messed around with the video equipment since they've been in here.'

William offered neither praise nor comment, and she glanced up to find him studying her, an unreadable expression on his face.

'Well?' she asked, feeling the silence between them tending towards uncomfortable.

'You have done a great job,' he said—too late with the praise. 'But now there's no excuse for us to eat together tonight.'

She stared blankly at him, trying to work out if he was serious. And if he was, then why.

One way to find out.

'Were you looking for an excuse?' she asked.

The scrutiny continued.

'I suppose I was. I've enjoyed our meals together.'

Not your company, she told herself. Just the meals, so don't go getting any ideas.

'So have I,' she admitted. 'But when I've been up since four and been run off my feet all day, a boiled egg with toast, followed by a deep bath and then an early night is my idea of heaven.'

'No date?' His eyebrows rose interrogatively. 'You've a work function tomorrow night, so when do you fit in your social life?'

The questions—particularly the first—made her uncomfortable, although she knew she shouldn't have to apologise for not having a social life.

'Hospital doctors on the lower rungs of the ladder don't have time for social lives,' she told him. 'That's why so many of them get married young—it saves having to keep apologising to angry boyfriends or girlfriends for being late, or standing them up because of an emergency, or abandoning them in pubs and picture theatres when they're bleeped. Wives and husbands are expected to understand.'

'You weren't tempted?' The aggravating man seemed intent on pursuing this subject. 'Didn't take that option?'

Very nearly, should have been the answer, but he didn't need to know that, so she said, 'No,' then lifted her wrist to look at her watch.

'Well, I'll see you Monday,' she added with false cheeriness, certain if she didn't escape, he'd pursue the subject.

'No, you won't,' he said, then he zapped a split-second version of the smile her way. 'At least, you probably will, but before then you'll see me tomorrow. I'm driving you out to Mark's, remember? I'll call by about seven. Does that suit you?'

As they'd already made the arrangement, she could hardly unmake it. And it *would* be stupid to take two cars. But common sense told her she should be seeing less of William Alexander, not more.

Dressing for the 'works party' brought its own set of problems. After a week of delightfully sunny spring, winter had returned with a vengeance. The day had been a nasty early April Fool's joke, cold, wet and windy.

Prue sifted through her wardrobe, wryly reflecting that people who had no social life had no need for 'going out' clothes. Her 'good' clothes, once smart, were slightly out of fashion now. Clothes she'd spent vast sums of money on in her hedonistic days with Paul. There was the sexy black dress she'd bought towards the end of their relationship—the dress she'd worn when he'd proposed, in fact.

Not quite the thing for Mark and Anna's.

And as for that red suit.

She had 'the skirt', of course. It predated even Paul. The kind of quality that never wore out. It was straight, long, and black. The perfect skirt, she'd once thought. A classic. With a shirt it could be casual, with a velvet top, formal.

Paul had hated it—or perhaps not hated it, but grown bored with seeing it. Every time they went out—in the beginning!

It's still a good skirt, Prue told herself, and she hauled it out of the cupboard and pulled off the encasing plastic.

Then remembered the sweater.

She'd bought it at the same sale as she'd bought the sunshiny yellow one, a thing of such elegant beauty she hadn't been able to resist. Then she'd tucked it away, knowing it might be years before she had an opportunity to wear it.

She pulled a chair over to her cupboard and reached into the back of the top shelf. It was there, still wrapped in tissue paper.

Loosely knitted in baby mohair, it was the softest, most touch-enticing garment she'd ever owned. Even now, unwrapping it on the bed, she had to stroke it. V-necked, long-sleeved, its only adornments were two long-stemmed rose-buds embroidered in the same dark blue wool, barely visible, but adding something special with their thicker texture.

Excitement began to filter through her body, tightening her nerves and making her feel more alert—more alive. She dressed quickly, and spent the extra time on make-up, high-lighting her eyes with dark liner and a silvery blue shadow, her cheeks with blusher, her lips with a gloss. Then, in honour of the sweater, she dug through her bathroom cab-inet, seeking the glittery stuff she'd bought last Christmas, when she and Crystal had dressed as fairies for the final therapy session of the year.

Just a little, the shop assistant had said, near your eyes, on your cheek-bones.

She smoothed on just a little and stood back to study the effect.

'You'll do,' she told herself as the buzzer sounded.

She hurried to the door to let William in downstairs, then grabbed her coat and pulled it on, hiding the beautiful sweater, concerned she might be overdressed.

Too late now.

Her stomach rolled uneasily. Not nervously, surely? she

thought as she opened her flat door, expecting to find William outside.

He wasn't there. The door must be playing up again.

'I'll be right down,' she called through the intercom, although she doubted that was working either. Picked up her handbag, still unsorted, locked her door and headed down the steps.

The stomach rolling increased, becoming almost full-scale panic when she opened the door to see a different William. Still suited, but tonight, in place of the light grey suit he often wore to work, he was in a dark charcoal-grey that looked almost black in the gloomy twilight.

'Your door-opening mechanism's not working,' he told her.

'I guessed it wasn't. That's why I came down.'

What a stupid conversation, her head yelled, but, with her stomach in revolt and her heart behaving oddly, she was pleased to find she could speak at all. She pulled her coat more tightly around her body.

'Shall we go?'

He looked surprised, as if she'd jolted him out of some deep contemplation of the meaning of the universe, then he said, 'Yes, yes, of course. You look very nice, you know.'

He spoke so quickly the words ran together, like a child's repetition of a nursery rhyme, or lesson.

'As all you can see of me is the oldest living Burberry in South Ken, I won't take that as a compliment.'

Again he seemed startled, peering at her as if to see if she was joking.

'I meant your face,' he added, when she didn't smile to let him off the hook. 'It's all aglow. Lit up. Very fetching.'

'It's not me,' she said, relenting. 'It's glittery make-up. I thought Mark's party warranted something special.'

'Ah!' he said, but still he studied her. Probably working out what muscles made the glitter sparkle most!

Discomfited by this scrutiny, Prue moved away, out of the protection of the front portico, walking carefully down the steps.

He produced an umbrella—from his capacious pocket?— and held it over her, taking her arm as she reached the last but one, supporting her and sending that warmth washing through her body.

'Over here. Mind the puddles. The car's old, but it runs well and it doesn't leak. At least, not on my side, and I assume not on the passenger side or Isobel would have complained about it. She was always on at me about buying something newer. In fact, she met her car salesman when trawling through the showrooms for something she'd have considered suitable for me to drive.'

'You in a Bentley?' Prue said in disbelief. 'And she'd known you eight years?'

'Silly, wasn't it?' William agreed, holding the umbrella awkwardly aloft while bending to unlock the door of an almost vintage Jaguar coupé. 'Too smooth by half, you have to be, to drive a Bentley. And she'd known me a lot longer than eight years. More like ten or twelve.'

'Blimey!' Prue muttered inelegantly. 'You really did rush things, didn't you?'

The introduction of Isobel into the conversation had made her stomach feel better but had lodged a wedge of discomfort in the middle of her chest. The fact that William mentioned his ex-fiancée so often must mean he still cared for her.

Not that it had anything to do with Prue.

No relationships.

No distractions.

No men.

She repeated what had become her mantra these days as she slipped into the passenger seat of his car. But if mantras were supposed to protect and comfort you, this one wasn't working.

Especially when he joined her in the car, and a street light threw his profile into dark relief. Definitely a man. And definitely a distraction.

But no relationship. She was okay there. Would thirty-three per cent earn a conceded pass?

'—do you think?'

It was obviously a question, but what had he asked while she had contemplated the appeal of strong male profiles backlit by street lamps?

'Going via Fulham Road,' he added, in the voice of a man who knew patience was essential in dealing with women.

'You're driving, you decide,' she said, deciding definite was the way to go in this situation. Then she wondered.

'Did Isobel always advise on road directions, as well as ordering your meals?'

He manoeuvred into a stream of slow-moving traffic, then glanced her way.

'Do I detect the scratch of a feline, in that dulcet remark?' he asked, and Prue, who did feel decidedly, though irrationally, antagonistic towards his ex-fiancée, felt embarrassment squirm in her stomach.

'Not at all,' she told him, with as much *élan* as she could muster. 'It's just she figures so much in your conversation I naturally thought she must have been the prime motivating force in your life. Food. Directions. Clothes? Was it her fair hand behind the purchase of that great suit you're wearing?'

'Do you like it?' he asked, in the mild tone she was beginning to realise hid whatever he was feeling. 'You're right, though. It was her choice. She refused to let me wear my good "meetings at work" suit to some wedding or other we attended.'

Prue had said it to tease him and he'd struck back at her with the simplicity of the truth.

The thought of William and the dear departed-to-a-car-salesman Isobel at a wedding—holding hands in the back pew, sighing as the bride walked down the aisle, thinking mushy thoughts—was all too much for her. She gave up on the conversation and turned her attention to the rain, sluicing across streets dangerously black and slick with the wetness, the car a capsule of warmth in the wild weather.

William drove carefully, not wanting to risk having to stop suddenly, and perhaps skid into the next lane. It took great concentration, as having Prue Valentine beside him in his car was distracting. At first it had been the blueness of her eyes, and that trick of widening them. Then the chuckle, usually accompanied by bells.

But right now he couldn't see the eyes, and she certainly wasn't chuckling, yet his body was as tense as a coiled spring, his muscles bunched beneath his skin—on full sexual alert because a woman he barely knew was beside him in the car.

She'd given no sign that she was interested in him, treating him as a temporary colleague, with the same light-hearted warmth she showed to patients and other staff.

And that was how he should be treating her.

'If you open the glove-box you'll find some other rhymes I've scribbled down. The interior light's not working, but if you want to put them in your handbag you can look at them later and use whatever you want.'

She leaned forward, and light from outside illuminated her profile, sending a shaft of longing deep into his body.

'Why the use of "you", William Alexander?' she demanded, taking the list and tucking it away. 'Wasn't this to be a joint project? Shouldn't that be "we"?'

Her stern voice confirmed his dismal thoughts about the lack of interest on her part. There was nothing happening here between them, no matter how arousing her profile might be.

Although…

She'd more or less admitted not having a social life…

No, it was impossible. He worked erratic hours himself and he was often called out to talk to parents whose child had recently been diagnosed with CF, or comfort those whose loved one had lost the battle.

'Isn't that the house?'

Prue's question brought him out of his foolish suppositions—which had reached a long way past their joint erratic hours.

'Thanks,' he said, checking his rear-view mirror, then swinging the car around in a U-turn. 'Mind on something else.'

'How unusual!' she said sweetly, and there was enough light in the car to see her smile.

'No lecture about lack of concentration? Keeping my mind on what I was doing when in control of a machine with the potential to kill?'

Prue turned to him, a startled look on her face.

'Isobel?' she asked, and he nodded, then met her smile with a wry grin of his own.

'Obviously her influence was more far-reaching than I realised,' he said, and Prue felt a feather of apprehension trickle like ice-water down her spine.

It doesn't matter who influences him, she told herself as she unlatched the door and pushed it open. Nor that he's still hung up on Isobel. It's none of your business.

No men, remember.

They walked up the path, close together so the umbrella offered shelter to them both. At the entry, William shook the trusty accessory and shut it, then set it in the stand with others.

'We'll all take home the wrong one later,' he said, so

gloomily she decided his had probably been a present from you-know-who!

Feeling glum, and decidedly un-partyish, Prue stepped into the foyer, waved to Mark who was calling a greeting from across the room, kissed Anna's cheek, then looked the other way while their hostess hugged William, uttering little cries of delight about how good it was to see him.

Prue undid her belt and buttons and began to haul the coat off. Firm hands halted her, lifting it effortlessly off her shoulders, helping her ease one arm out, and then the other.

'That's beautiful. So soft to touch. I may be mauling you all night.'

William's voice was husky, his touch on her sweater feather-light.

'I liked the feel of it. That's why I bought it,' she managed to reply, moving aside as Anna greeted more guests.

Her voice had come out croaky, but that was nothing to how her insides felt with William stroking first her back and then her arm and shoulder.

'Beautiful,' he repeated, but this time he was in front of her and looking at her face.

'Oh, William! I had no idea you'd be here! You wonderful, wonderful man. How are you? Where's Isobel?'

The loud cries of delight shattered the moment. Prue stepped back further as a tall, sun-tanned blonde flung herself into William's arms.

By staying close to the wall, Prue was able to edge into the big drawing room where familiar faces banished her sudden feeling of loneliness.

'It's Nicole Barclay—Crystal's sister-in-law. Nikki Campbell she is now. She was the physio on the unit before Annette. Married this gorgeous Australian doctor and took off for down under. She must be back in England for some family occasion, because she's with Peter and Crystal.'

Pat explained all this as the newcomers entered the room.

Nicole's arm was tucked into William's where Prue's had been a couple of nights ago.

'She's very good-looking,' Prue said glumly.

'And very married,' Pat said, making Prue realise how much she'd given away with her comment. 'She was about six months pregnant when she came back for a visit in October, so there's a baby somewhere. Maybe that's why she's here. She's brought him home to meet her folks.'

Pat waved to the young woman, who gave a cry of delight and rushed forward to hug the unit nurse. Prue, knowing they'd have a lot to catch up on, moved away.

'Can I get you a drink? I'll get something for myself as well. That and a savoury should keep my hands occupied and off your body.'

William had materialised beside her.

She nodded yes to the drink, yes again to wine, all the while battling an urge to say how much she'd liked his hands on her.

When he returned to her side with wine for her and mineral water for himself, she sipped thirstily at the cool refreshment, then slowed down, knowing getting tipsy would make things worse, not better.

'We should circulate, I guess,' she said, looking out across the crowd of guests and wishing social obligations didn't include mixing in. 'Apart from the unit staff, Mark's obviously included staff from the wards our patients use most regularly. You'd know Holly and Ben Harvey from General Medical—have you run across Claudia and Lucas Morrison? Lucas is an orthopaedic consultant at Lizzie's, but the pair of them took off for foreign parts shortly after their wedding. They're back for a short holiday.'

She'd just finished this explanation when Lucas bore down on them.

'William, just the man I want to see. Rumour has it

you're working on deep muscles in the back and larger joints. Now—'

'Let's leave them to it,' Claudia said, taking Prue's arm and leading her away. 'We'll find somewhere to sit down and talk about clothes, or shops or food. You have no idea how much I miss the simple pleasures like popping into a shop for a loaf of bread, or browsing in clothes shops even when I have no intention of shopping.'

They talked clothes, and shops, but soon veered back to work, to the demands of working hospital hours and trying to fit it all in.

'We both want to start a family as soon as we come home for good,' Claudia said, 'but I worry if it's fair on kids when we're both likely to be working unstructured hours. I should have been a dermatologist. No one ever calls them out in the middle of the night to patch up the breakages from a car accident.'

'But would you have enjoyed it?' Prue asked. 'Would it have made you happy?'

'No!' Claudia replied in a doom-laden voice. 'And if I wasn't happy I'd be a rotten parent anyway. Well, wouldn't I?'

Prue didn't answer, too struck by the concept that an unhappy parent might be worse than one working awkward hours. She wanted to be alone to think this through—to see how it fitted with the big decision she'd taken when she'd decided to specialise.

'At least Lucas agrees with me,' Claudia was saying. 'He's happy for me to work, and says when the time comes and we do have a family, we'll do what other working couples do and have a nanny. Not that I know much about nannies, apart from what I've heard. I don't suppose you had a nanny? Have some first-hand experience you'd like to pass on?'

Prue was wondering how to answer, or avoid answering,

when a warm hand descended onto her shoulder and gave a little stroke.

'I thought I'd lost you. I've told Lucas I refuse to talk shop at a party. Now, come on, I want you to meet Nikki.'

Saved by the bell—or by William in this case!

Prue excused herself to Claudia and stood up, yielding her place on the sofa to Crystal. Let her and Claudia thrash out the problems of child care. Having decided not to have kids, Prue reminded herself, the issue didn't arise.

'Well, that was a pleasant evening,' William said as they walked back down the path much later. The rain had eased and he held his furled umbrella in one hand. He'd put her coat around her shoulders, but had kept his other hand inside it somehow so his fingers teased against the softness of the wool, firing the sensors in her skin with the feather-light caress.

It's the softness of the wool that's got him going, Prue reminded herself.

Distracted by the touch, Prue stumbled, the heel of one shoe stuck between the flagstones of the path. William caught her in his arms to steady her, and when he looked down into her eyes she couldn't quite believe it was just the wool.

Then his head dipped towards her, his lips claimed hers, and she knew it wasn't just the wool.

The kiss was sweet and hot—as intoxicating as a Christmas toddy—yet nothing more than a preliminary exploration of lips on lips, a tentative touch of tongue on tongue.

Prue's mind went blank as her physical self filled with a feverish delight, heat seeping through her veins and sending ripples of sensation to the furthermost parts of her body.

A loud whistle pierced the air, flinging her and William

apart, as embarrassment vied with confusion for top billing in her head.

'Bells and lights and whistles,' William muttered, settling her coat again around her shoulders and steering her firmly through the gate and along the footpath towards his car.

'I can't believe we did that!' Prue had some muttering of her own to do. And, judging by the irritability she was feeling, that was just the beginning.

'We were in the shadow of that rowan bush. Whoever whistled couldn't possibly have seen who we were,' William told her, but he didn't sound too certain about it. Nor did she know quite how to take his remark.

Did he not want to be recognised kissing her?

And if not, why not?

She had an excuse for her mortification. She didn't want to put up with the teasing and gossip at the unit. But William would be gone in a couple of weeks, so the talk couldn't matter to him.

'It was all your fault!'

She was muttering again, venting spleen with the childish accusation.

'Well, I like that,' he countered. 'If you hadn't worn that slinky, seductive sweater, I wouldn't have been tempted. And, anyway, you kissed me back.'

'That's not the point,' Prue told him crossly, unable to deny that her lips had clung to his with all the desperation of a drowning man to a life-raft. 'And I don't think it's much of a compliment to tell a woman you only kissed her because you liked the feel of her sweater.'

He sighed and she guessed he was probably rolling his eyes heavenward as well. Then he put his hands on her shoulders and turned her to face him.

'Shall we try again?' he suggested, a smile lurking in the depths of his eyes. 'Under the street light where we're easily recognisable. My hands on your Burberry, not your sweater. Do it because it felt good, and I think we both enjoyed it?'

Prue's knees began to shake, and her heart thumped in a fast, heavy rhythm. Her breathing went awry and her arms ached to reach out and hold him, to try the kiss again to see if it could possibly have been as riveting as she remembered it.

'Perhaps we'd better not,' she croaked, forcing the words out past the objections of her body. 'I'm really busy at the moment, don't need, want, complications, relationships, men in my life.'

The words tripped and stumbled and she knew she hadn't sounded very convincing when he moved closer.

'I'm not talking about complications, or relationships, or even men,' he said evenly. 'I'm talking about a kiss, Prue Valentine. One kiss. That's all.'

And against all her good intentions, the repetition of her mantra, and her stock of common sense, she raised her head, and when his lips touched hers she welcomed them with all the fire that had flamed inside her earlier, matching his intensity with her own—betraying all her brave words with her ardour.

Until a passing car driver flashed his headlights at them, and she drew away, shaken and embarrassed.

CHAPTER TEN

THEY drove home in silence, William confused about so many things, not least of which was what his passenger was thinking. It was the lights and bells and whistles throwing him, he finally decided. The stupid suggestion Isobel had implanted in his head.

Once he got past that and analysed this attraction coolly, logically and rationally, he'd be able to deal with it. An affair would probably be the best way to go. Something clean and simple. No strings. No expectations beyond the pleasure they could share. They were both mature, intelligent adults. Surely they could work out what to do about what was obviously a strong physical attraction.

'Are you working tomorrow?' he asked as he turned off Fulham Road, and headed into the rabbit warren of streets leading to Prue's flat.

'I've some reading I have to do and, if I have any spare time, it will be spent sleeping,' she said, firmly enough to let him know he wasn't going to figure in any of her plans.

'Perhaps dinner?' he asked hopefully, not feeling quite so mature as an almost adolescent uncertainty gripped his intestines.

'I don't think so,' she replied, her eyes on the road ahead, her voice as cool as the rain still falling outside.

'Well, I suppose we can catch up on Monday at work,' he muttered, pulling up outside her flat, double parking because he'd already driven once around the gardens and failed to find a space. 'Or at lunch-time for a run,' he added hopefully

'In this weather?'

He took heart from her voice, which was light and teasing.

'We could go to the gym,' he offered quickly. 'Or have a swim.'

She turned towards him now and put a hand on his arm.

'Let's wait and see,' she said softly. 'Thank you for driving me. It was a lovely evening.'

He tried to see her eyes, wanted to kiss her again, knew things were all wrong, but hadn't a clue how to make them right. Nothing in his relationship with Isobel had prepared him for this uncertainty.

'I'll see you Monday,' she added, then she unlatched the door and got out, shutting it behind her, then dashing through the drizzle towards the shelter of the entrance.

By the time he'd pulled himself together enough to get out of the car, she had the front door open and the security light was on in the foyer. She turned, backlit again, slim, elegant, beautiful—and walking away from him.

'Don't get out,' she called, although he already was. 'If you leave the car there someone's sure to want it moved.'

Then the door closed behind her, shutting out the light.

In more ways than one.

The cool, rational, logical thinking didn't seem to work and by Monday he was so tense when he met her in the car park he blurted out the first thing on his mind.

Well, it was the second and the third as well, and probably down to seventeenth thing if anyone was counting.

'How would you feel about an affair?'

'No, thanks,' she said, so casually offhand he wanted to strangle her.

'You could at least give a reason,' he said, following her towards the lift that would take them up into the building.

'Why?' she asked, turning to face him and using those wide blue eyes to add an extra challenge to the words.

'Because,' he blustered, struggling to find a word or two to follow that lame beginning. But not succeeding.

She laughed, but he knew the bells he heard were something to do with hospital routine, not her laugh at all. Coincidence, that was all it was. At least he'd got that far with his cool, rational, et cetera.

'I've a ward round,' she said, in the huskily compassionate voice he'd heard her use to patients. 'We can catch up later. And thanks for the rhymes. They were great.'

'Added as a sop for my pride, no doubt,' he growled to himself as she tap tapped her way down the corridor.

Tap-tapped? Did she always wear heels that high? Or was her skirt shorter than usual? Whatever the difference, it made the most of shapely legs he hadn't really noticed before. Too caught up with the whole person.

But now he looked…

He could imagine those legs twining with his, wrapping around his back—

'Lusting after my junior, Will?'

Mark's voice startled him, while the question made him burn with shame.

He'd been doing exactly that!

'We were discussing the Easter Egg Hunt,' he said stiffly, knowing Prue wouldn't want gossip about what was—or wasn't, as it turned out—going on between them.

'Ah,' said Mark. 'I thought that must be it. Saw you discussing it on my path on Saturday night as well. You know, I really admire your dedication to duty.'

He punched William lightly on the shoulder and walked on, changing the subject to work-related matters. William walked with him, grappling with Mark's words as he switched from confused would-be lover to professional again.

By lunch-time, he was feeling wrung out. The morning therapy session had dragged, unhappy parents had complained about the stress of coping with their child's illness *and* having to do daily exercise routines, and one curly-haired moppet had climbed onto his knee, for the specific purpose, it seemed, of throwing up all over him. He was now working in his track suit, and seriously reviewing his unorthodox policy of yearly hands-on physio to keep him on the ball.

'Ah, I thought I might have missed you. I know I complain all the time I'm running but I've decided it's really good for me and if I get into the habit while you're here, I just might keep it up.'

He looked up from the file he'd been pretending to read and stared at the apparition in the doorway.

Not only was Prue here, but she was dressed in her blue track suit and running shoes, and had a large golf umbrella clutched in one hand.

'You did say you ran in all weather,' she added, uncertainty creeping into her voice.

'I didn't—I thought—'

'I could fill you in on the Easter Egg Hunt,' she continued, as if trying to persuade him to accompany her. The thought made his heart lurch but when she said, 'Kick-off is at two if you're anywhere near a television,' he had to wonder if perhaps talking about the Hunt *was* all she wanted.

Grappling with too many conflicting emotions immobilised him, and in the end it was Pat's, 'Why are you dithering?' that saved him.

'I don't dither,' he said frostily, pushing his chair back and standing up straight to add height to his injured dignity.

He nodded to Prue.

'Well, I'm ready,' he said. 'Let's go.'

'Have you got your umbrella?' she asked. 'I mean, I know mine's big, but jogging? Wouldn't one of us get drips down the back of the neck?'

He grabbed his umbrella from the stand and followed her out the door, turning back to scowl at Pat who was laughing at some private joke.

The distance between the umbrellas precluded any conversation—about rabbits or anything else—while they ran.

'I've a wardsman happy to wear the rabbit suit,' Prue told him when they slowed for the walk home and conversation was easier. 'Nick Jones has his introduction worked out—a fast breaking news story about a strange rabbit loose in the hospital. He's going to do the intrepid reporter act, tracking down the intruder and demanding to know what's going on.'

'And do you have a clue in place?' William asked, although he didn't want to talk about clues or rabbits or anything but how he felt and what he was supposed to do about it now she'd said no thanks to an affair.

'I will have by then,' she said, with a smile that made him wish she'd answered differently. To the affair, not his more recent question. 'First the rabbit has to confess to Nick he's lost his eggs, and one of the children will offer him a rugby ball and ask if that will do because it's egg-shaped.'

She stopped and turned towards him, the smile now sparkling in her eyes.

'The teachers have got right behind it, and they're already planning on making or finding a lot of egg-shaped objects to offer to him when he visits different wards.'

'And where's the clue?' William persisted, because talking to her about the Easter treat was preferable to not talking to her at all.

'It's in a balloon. When he doesn't want the rugby ball, another child will offer an egg-shaped balloon, and he'll burst it accidentally, find the clue, read it out—it's your light and buzzer one—and go searching around the ward with the children encouraging him and the video camera recording it all.'

She paused as if marshalling her thoughts.

'Once he's found the clue by the console, it will lead him to the next ward—actually down to Outpatients; your coming and going clue—where he'll be at two tomorrow.'

'Complete with the camera crew and interviewer!' William was sufficiently impressed to forget about his own dilemma and add, 'It sounds wonderful. Congratulations. I might be pretending to Mark to be part of it, but it was all your idea.'

She turned away, continued walking, but he thought he could detect a flush of colour in her clear skin, a sudden darkening of those eleven pale freckles.

Had his praise pleased her so much?

Or was it the unspoken things going on between them, the silent messages of his body to hers, that had affected her.

As he had predicted, the televising of the rabbit's arrival, his loud wails of despair over losing his eggs, the children's attempts to soothe him, and the finding of the first clue, was an outstanding success.

'The cardiac ward phoned through to ask when the rabbit was due up there. The staff there will bring in some real eggs so the patients can dye them and offer them to the rabbit, and Orthopaedics are going to make eggs from plaster and paint them,' Pat told him when he returned to the unit after a meeting with Prue and the rabbit to discuss the next day's adventure.

'Will you let Prue know?' Pat added, and William agreed, but felt uncomfortable. Partly because he wasn't sure he liked the way Pat took it for granted he'd see her, but mostly because 'letting Prue know' might seem, to Prue, an excuse to foist himself on her again.

In the end, it was she who contacted him, although he who suggested dinner together.

'Well, I'm paying,' she said, and his heart beat out a tap-dance of relief. 'I can't keep letting you pay out of some misguided sense of chivalry. I mean, it's only business and I want to pick your brains.'

They agreed to meet in the coffee shop as Prue was on first call and didn't want to be too far away.

'See,' she said, halfway through the meal when she was bleeped and had to excuse herself. 'It's a good thing we were only discussing work; social lives are impossible. Will you think about the clue for Chests? I'd like it coughy and wheezy if possible, but I've been racking my brains and come up with nothing. I don't think rhyming couplets are my forte.'

He watched her whisk away, and told himself that, at least until Easter, he had some place in her life.

'I'll be glad when Easter's over,' Prue told herself, on the Thursday of the following week. Three days to go and still no clue to lead the rabbit to the chest clinic. Somehow she'd managed to keep a professional distance between her-self and William, but working on the rabbit's hunt—and relying on William's agile brain for clues—had meant they'd spent a lot of time together.

Time that put a strain on her determination not to get involved. On her decision to remain focussed on her work.

Running with him was one thing. She knew she should keep that up because she *was* feeling fitter. More alive, somehow. And although running had some problems, such as when she'd tripped on the edge of the gutter one day and he'd caught her in his arms and looked into her eyes, most times she was too busy breathing to worry about the attraction that ate into her body whenever he was near.

But planning, laughing over his nonsensical rhymes, delighting in his sense of the ridiculous—that was seductive stuff and the sooner it was over with, the better.

She was making her way towards the ward, so lost in her thoughts she bumped into Gareth Davies, the hospital's top plastic surgeon.

'I was looking for you,' he said, steadying her with a hand on her shoulder as his wife, Peggie, joined them. 'I noticed you'd introduced a couple of new reporters to the team and wondered if we could include one of my lot. Kelly Shaw's undergoing facial reconstruction after an accident. It's been a long series of operations for the youngster and she's coming through it quite well, but I know she'd get a kick out of being involved.'

Prue hesitated.

Peggie was looking anxiously at her, as if this was important to both the doctors as well as their patient.

Every child in the hospital wanted to get more directly involved, and choosing those to include had been difficult.

'Perhaps she could have a special part,' she suggested. 'On Easter Sunday I'd planned to have the rabbit find the eggs in the small day theatre, as that won't be in use over the holiday period. Could we dress her up as a fairy, perhaps, make her the guardian of the eggs?'

'A fairy would be perfect!' Peggie said, clapping her hands together with delight. 'I've a swirly multi-coloured skirt I can make into a dress, and fairy wings seem to be on sale at every second shop these days. Same time Sunday? Two o'clock?'

Prue smiled at Peggie's enthusiasm and nodded, while Peggie quietened her husband's protest that they'd agreed to keep away from the hospital over the Easter weekend.

'Of course we have to come in,' Peggie said, then added wistfully, 'In fact, I've been rather hoping I might get called in on the other days as well. I hate to think I'm going to miss the last few showings of the Great Easter Egg Hunt.'

Gareth reached out and ruffled his hand through his wife's hair, a gesture so affectionately intimate Prue felt a stab of loneliness in the region of her heart.

'We'll come in,' he promised her, 'though the way the news of what's happening here has spread, you might be able to catch it on the BBC.' He looked at Prue. 'It was a grand idea and it has the whole hospital talking. Where does he go next?'

'He was in Cardiology today,' Prue replied, 'then Oncology on Good Friday. I chose that because none of the kids will be having radiology that day so they can all join in—then, if I can think up a clue to get him to Chests, he's there on Saturday. The staff there have all kinds of surprises planned, although, after the kids in Orthopaedics glued their hands together making plaster eggs, surprises aren't as popular with the management as they might have been.'

'We heard about that,' Peggie said. 'Plastics' offerings of lemons and avocados and aubergines as egg substitutes were fairly tame after that grand gesture.'

'I thought you showed great initiative,' Prue told her. 'And the rabbit had really got into his stride by then and threw a beautiful tantrum.'

They were all laughing about it when footsteps sounded behind Prue and alert nerve-endings down her spine told her it was William.

'Here's the man responsible for the clues,' she said, introducing him to the other couple.

'And for putting that sparkle in your eyes, I believe,' Peggie teased, her lilting Irish voice robbing the words of offence.

But lack of offence didn't stop Prue flushing, so much heat creeping into her cheeks she knew a denial would be pointless.

'All lies and innuendo,' William said firmly. 'We're just good friends.'

He might have carried it off, too, Prue thought, if he hadn't put his arm around her shoulders at the same time, and tucked her close into his body—radiating more heat than warmth this time.

'That's what we thought,' Peggie said, her smile mocking the words. 'Well, if I've a fairy costume to make, we'd best be off.'

Prue bit her tongue until they were out of earshot, then spun to face her tormentor.

'Why did you go and do that?' she demanded, furious with herself, and him, and hospital gossip in general.

'Do what?' he said, the dark eyes so guileless she had to choke back a snort of disbelief. 'Tell them there was nothing in it? There isn't, is there?'

She wanted to stamp her foot and howl with frustration.

'You might have said that, but you put your arm around me,' she reminded him, her rage making her breathless. 'Eight years?' she huffed. 'You'd last about eight minutes with me. That Isobel was a martyr to have put up with you for so long.'

She saw the muscle move in his cheek and knew he was holding back a grin.

Which made her angrier, but what could she do? Slug him one in the corridor outside the ward? Kick him in the shins?

'Is this a bad time to tell you I've come up with a clue for Chests?' His voice made the words seductive. He was still teasing her, but if he'd found a solution to her problem she'd have to shelve the violence—at least until he'd parted with the clue.

'You have?' Suspicion edged her voice.

He gave a shrug and a little self-deprecatory smile that wouldn't have fooled a two-year-old.

'I think it will do!' he said, then he folded his hands in front of his chest like a child reciting a poem, smiled down at her and said,

'Where you go with coughs and sneezes,
    In the place for whoops and wheezes,
    Atomisers, nebulisers, masks and tubes and tanks,
    Ask the kids who use them most, and don't forget your
thanks.'

Prue tried not to laugh, but William's best wounded expression broke her up completely.

'It's terrible,' she said, nearly choking as she tried to talk and chuckle at the same time. 'Terrible!'

'It won't do?' he asked, managing to look more wounded than ever.

'Of course it will do,' she told him, bending over to catch her breath and control the laughter, then straightening up to look into his deep-set eyes. 'The kids will love it! You're a genius! Thank you, William!'

She put her arms around him and gave him a hug, her rage forgotten in her gratitude for this man who cared enough to make things special for the hospital's young patients.

'Very touching, but are hospital corridors quite the right place for such carryings-on? As I remember, you took a dim view of public displays of affection, Prudence. Something to do with your name, no doubt.'

William's arms had just closed around her—purely to return the hug, she was sure—when she heard Paul's voice.

Her immediate reaction was to wish for invisibility—or, failing that, if Lent was off-season for miracles, to remain with her head buried against William's chest.

Which wouldn't work either, she realised, all within a split second of being caught.

She eased out of William's comforting clasp and faced the man she'd once thought she might marry.

'Hello, Paul. What brings you to Lizzie's?'

She hoped she sounded more at ease than she felt, her body rigid with the dual tension of having Paul's presence in front of her, William's behind.

Paul looked her up and down and she knew he was registering the contrast in their appearance. And possibly wondering what he'd ever seen in her. He, of course, was immaculate as ever, while she was at the end of a long day and decidedly scruffy.

'I've a patient here,' he replied. 'She was transferred across during the fumes debacle, then deteriorated to the extent it was decided to keep her here.'

Prue nodded. She'd heard about the young leukaemia patient who'd remained with them.

'How's she doing?'

It was the natural question to ask, but asked more from fear of the silences hovering between them than for information about the patient she didn't know.

'She'll pull through. This time,' he said.

Prue, who knew that, for all his funny ways, he cared deeply about his patients, touched him on the arm and said, 'I'm glad.'

He shook her hand off as if her touch might contaminate him, and when she raised startled eyes to his she saw a blaze of anger so bright she flinched.

The word 'why' hovered on her lips but Paul was no longer looking at her, his angry gaze directed over her shoulder at William.

'I'd heard she had a new man on a string,' Paul said, his tone almost conversational, though laced with bitterness. 'I wouldn't try too hard to get her into bed. She's just as cold and uptight there as she is out of it.'

Prue was battling the effect of this sudden and unprovoked attack when a large strong hand clamped down on one shoulder and she was drawn back until her body rested against William's chest.

'Was that your experience?' the lovely tenor voice drawled, while William's hand left her shoulder and his arm wrapped around her torso, holding her to him.

'I don't usually discuss my sex life in the corridors of the hospital but in this case I'll make an exception,' William continued in the same flat tone. 'If I were you I'd look to yourself if something was lacking in your relationship with Prue, because she is, without doubt, the warmest, most generous, giving, sexy and seductive woman I've ever had the pleasure to know. Then there's her sensuous inventiveness in bed, her sheer delight in every aspect of our sexual relationship. Not that it stops there. Oh, no, that's just icing on the cake.'

He stopped his dissertation long enough to press a kiss behind Prue's ear, and give a deep chuckle. Then he added, in a husky whisper, loud enough for Paul to hear, 'Remember the icing *off* the cake.'

She might have been embarrassed earlier when William had put his arm around her shoulders, but, if that was the case, embarrassed didn't begin to describe how Prue felt now!

Paul was staring at William with a look of such disbelief on his face it was almost comical.

'Well, d-don't expect her to stay home and look after the children,' he stuttered. 'She's far too obsessed about her glorious career, far too selfish to consider *their* welfare.'

He spun on his heel and stormed off, leaving Prue weak with relief—sagging against William's hard, strong body.

'Do you have many children that you've abandoned out of selfishness?' he asked, and, totally overcome by the emotional stress of Paul's attack, and the temptations of William's body, Prue burst into tears.

William thought he'd reacted splendidly to this new crisis, steering his weeping colleague into a storeroom so she could rid herself of moisture in peace, even finding a large face cloth on one of the shelves to mop at the tears.

At least, he'd thought it a face cloth but it must have been scratchy, for his charge stopped crying for long enough to demand, 'What's this?'

More familiar with the hospital, and apparently with storerooms, she snapped on a light, looked at the cloth in her hand, and the tears switched to laughter.

He was considering treatment for hysteria when she collapsed onto an upturned bucket, and, still chuckling, looked up at him.

'Oh, William, you were wonderful,' she said. 'I nearly died at the time, but now I think about it, I'm so glad you told him off. But inventive? Why ever did you say that? And what could we possibly have been doing with cake icing?'

He was about to make several suggestions when she sobered, and he realised, with a little pang of loss in his heart, that she'd remembered they were no more than colleagues.

He squatted down in front of her.

'We could do whatever you wish with icing,' he said softly. 'And how could you not be inventive with the active and adventurous mind you've got? How could you not be generous and giving and all the other things I said, when it's in your nature—an essential part of who you are.'

She looked embarrassed, then confused, then woebegone, her blue eyes gazing into his with a piteous intensity.

He pressed a finger against her lips.

'Not a word,' he said. 'Let's get out of here. The cupboard and the hospital. I'll take you home—you shouldn't be driving while you're still shaken by that imbecile. You can have a nice relaxing bath, get changed into something comfortable, then I'll take you on to my place and cook you dinner. How does that sound?'

It sounded wonderful.

Too wonderful?

'Paul was right,' she said slowly. 'I *am* committed to my career, but it wasn't about staying home to mind children that we argued, it was having children in the first place.'

'Aren't we getting ahead of ourselves here?' William asked, his eyes dark with concern for her.

Prue shook her head, refusing to give in to dark concerned eyes.

'No! I have to get it said. I didn't see it as leading Paul on, but he obviously took it that way to say what he did today. To be so bitter after more than a year. I'd always thought he knew how I felt, and that he understood why.'

She paused, gathering all her resources to see her through the explanation she knew she owed to William. She lifted her head to watch his face as she explained, hoping to read his reaction in his eyes.

'The Wells family dynamics upset me because it echoed my family. My mother, who was a brilliant biologist, was everything Paul called me—cool and distant, obsessed with her career. When my nanny, whom I adored, left, my father went with her.'

William's hands closed over hers and the understanding in his eyes almost undid her.

'So you lost the two people who showed you affection? What happened after that? Who cared for you then?'

Prue shrugged, battling his understanding more than the past.

'Dailies. People who came in to clean and cook until I went to boarding-school.' She forced a smile. 'It sounds worse than it was. I had a happy enough life, William, but it did affect me. To the extent that when it came time to decide whether or not I'd specialise, I had to look ahead and think through the implications.'

She met his eyes.

'I'm good at what I do,' she told him, 'and I know I have a lot to offer. But to specialise, and keep working, then have a family which would be primarily raised by an outsider—for me that wasn't an option.'

'Paul didn't understand that?' William asked and Prue smiled at the understatement.

'Paul understood all right. He was kind enough to tell me, when we were shredding each other's feelings for the final time, that he'd particularly chosen me because of my attitude to children—or to children being brought up by nannies or au pairs. He'd taken it to mean I'd give up my work to stay home with the children, to run his house, entertain for him, probably lick his boots from time to time.'

Prue heard remembered anger creep into her voice, and laughed it away.

'Actually, I realised later I'd probably have done all those things for him if I'd really loved him—'

'Even boot-licking?' William asked, the smile that lurked around his lips also dancing in his eyes.

'Probably!' she admitted. 'What made me so mad was his attitude that, while his career was paramount, mine wasn't. I hadn't ever thought of myself as a career woman until then, but when he spoke that way I felt resentful, and angry, and very hot and bothered.'

William touched her cheek.

'Of course you would. As you said, you're too good at what you do to give it up.'

His agreement, softly—even tenderly—spoken, tore at Prue's heart. He understands we can't go on, she realised. Can't ever find out if we'd be good in bed together—if I'd be sensual and inventive.

And *she'd* never know about the icing.

CHAPTER ELEVEN

'OH, EXCUSE me. I didn't realise this storeroom was occupied.'

Prue shot to her feet as the wardsman opened the door.
She stumbled over William who was still squatting on the
floor. They landed in a tangle of mops, limbs, buckets and
embarrassment.

'We were talking, nothing more,' Prue told the grinning
man as she struggled to her feet, then helped William up.

'I'd believe you, love, though millions wouldn't,' the
wardsman said. 'You all right there?'

He asked the question of William, who was trying to
disentangle his foot from the mop-squeezing mechanism on
a bucket.

'I hope to be,' William told him, and Prue, thinking he
might have injured himself, dropped to her knees to help.

'Boot-licking yet?' William's huskily teasing question
froze her fingers and she looked up to see a strange expression on his face. As if he was listening to distant noises,
seeing things she couldn't see.

'Releasing your foot,' she told him, with as much cool
control as she could muster after that strange expression
had done even stranger things to her internal organs.

'Ah,' he said, which in itself meant nothing. It was the
satisfaction in his voice that bothered her.

With William freed, Prue stood up, then, telling herself
appearance was everything, she assumed what she hoped
was an expression of calm dignity and stepped out of the
storeroom.

A young nurse hurrying past threw her a questioning

look, the wardsman, smiling to himself, began to set his pails and brooms to rights, and William, still looking dazed, emerged and glanced around as if trying to work out where he was.

'This way,' Prue said, and set off briskly towards the lifts. Now they were back in public she was embarrassed to think she'd told William so much. And from the tension she could feel between them, he wasn't happy about being the recipient.

Best to get it sorted out now, before her silly cupboard confession became a huge barrier between them.

She pressed the button to summon the lift, then looked up at him, into eyes that hid his thoughts.

'I'm sorry to have poured out all that angst over you,' she said, as casually as she could. 'Just your bad luck being in the wrong place at the wrong time.'

He nodded, but said nothing. Nor did he smile, though she searched his face for that tell-tale twitch at the corner of his mobile lips, searched his eyes for the smile that usually lurked there.

And, when she didn't find either, her heart gave a little clutch of panic, as if she'd lost something precious.

The lift arrived and they stepped inside—temporary colleagues who had shared a little of each other's lives as they shared a corner of the cluttered space in this metal cube.

'Do you have to come into work to organise the rabbit over the holiday break?' William asked, as the lift stopped and more passengers got on.

'I'm on duty tomorrow and Saturday,' Prue told him, aware of his body heat in spite of a good six inches' space between them. 'On call the other two days so it's no problem coming in.'

'Have the eggs arrived?'

She wanted to yell at him, to tell him he didn't have to

make polite conversation—that silence was just fine with her.

'Yes!' she muttered, since yelling didn't seem to be an option in a crowded lift. Then she realised what working over the holiday break meant. She was free next week— four whole days off. Four days—no, eight, if you counted the Easter holiday weekend—when she wouldn't have to see William, wouldn't have to act polite—wouldn't have to run!

She was so relieved she smiled at him and even said a polite goodbye when they parted on the ground floor.

So his appearance, in a smart dark green track suit, the following day, threw her out completely. She was lying on a couch in the doctors' mess, her feet propped on the arm, lazily perusing a recent medical magazine but not taking in much of the information.

'You're not ready for your run,' he said, face still impassive and unreadable.

'It's a holiday weekend—why aren't you holidaying somewhere? Isle of Wight, Seville, Paris?'

'I have a project,' he told her, then he did almost smile as he added, 'Three, in fact, with you, the rabbit and Mark's communication paper. The last we can work on next week, but I could hardly give up on your fitness, or leave you here to handle rabbit-mania on your own. Did Mark tell you the press are coming this afternoon? Martyn Lennard decided it might be good PR for the hospital and invited them to see some action.'

Prue stared at him, then down at the T-shirt she'd worn to cheer herself up. Her friend Melissa had given it to her when she and Paul had broken up and it read, 'Not all men are annoying. Some are dead.'

She buttoned her white coat over it, then realised William seemed to be waiting for something.

'We're running, remember,' he said. 'I assume your gear

is here. Get changed, we haven't got all day.' He paused, then smiled at her. 'Well, I have,' he corrected himself, 'so maybe we can lunch afterwards. You don't look as if you're rushed off your feet.'

Unable to think of an immediate excuse for not running, Prue slid her feet to the floor and straightened to a sitting position. It didn't help her thought processes one bit. William's arrival—the sight of him standing in the door-way—had scrambled her brain.

'Come on,' he urged. 'On your feet. A brisk run in the fresh air is just what you need to perk you up a bit.'

'Perk me up a bit?' Prue grumbled, although she did stand up. 'What a revolting expression!'

William smiled, totally unrepentant.

The smile started such a chain reaction of sensation through her body, she decided maybe fresh air *would* be good. At least while she ran, with breathing such a priority, she wouldn't notice smiles. She crossed to her locker, hauled out her running gear, and headed for the bathroom.

Would he say something about her 'true confession' ep-isode in the storeroom?

Should she apologise again or just hope he'd already forgotten it?

Not that she could imagine a man of his intelligence forgetting much. In fact, his head seemed to be such a cor-nucopia of disparate information, she doubted he'd ever forgotten anything.

Though she could hope…

Hope lasted until they had crossed the road, very quiet on this public holiday, and were jogging through the park.

'So, where's your mother? Do you see her? Have a good relationship with her now you're an adult? And your father? Did he stay in touch?'

Prue ran faster, but knew she'd have to answer. Or he'd keep asking—keep prodding away at the hidden compartments in her mind until the locks broke open and she told him what he wanted to know.

'My mother lives in London, and, yes, I see her, but not often.'

She glanced towards William, wondering if that would do. It was an answer, after all.

His, 'And?' answered her thoughts.

'We don't have a close relationship,' Prue replied, then decided she might as well tell the whole sorry story. She stopped running and turned to face him. 'For all her brilliance, she didn't handle being on her own too well and remarried, probably too quickly. When that didn't work, she had a couple of lovers who moved in and then moved out. Then, when I finished school and we might have become closer, she fell in love. Really in love. She's still with that man.'

'Which left you on the outside once again,' William said, compassion deepening his voice, softening his dark eyes.

Softening her heart!

'I don't need your pity, William Alexander,' she said stoutly. 'As I said, I had a happy childhood. I went to a great school, made friends I still see today, got on with life and made the most of it.'

And to show him, she began to run again, not too fast in case he got some weird idea she was running away from the past.

'And your father?'

'He's in Canada, and, I suppose, if birthday and Christmas cards constitute keeping in touch, then, yes, he did. I've been over to visit him and Brita, met my half-sisters and half-brother. We're a totally civilised non-nuclear family.'

William ran easily beside her, his heart rate raised more by Prue's presence by his side than by the exercise. There were no flashing lights, no bells, no whistles, but what he felt for her must surely be love.

Why else would stories of her childhood make his gut ache?

Why else would the thought of the small Prue heading off to nursery school with her mother's daily make him hot with anger?

And as for the adolescent Prue, leaving the security of boarding-school for a home where no one wanted her. It made him mad enough for murder.

He swallowed the thickness in his throat and must have accelerated, a plaintive, 'Hey, since when did this become a race?' pulling him up short.

He slowed his pace and tried to think.

Common sense told him not to rush her, but instinct suggested time wouldn't help.

'I've always intended working from home at some stage of my life,' he said, blurting out the words in his haste to get them said. 'I've notes for a book I'll never get written while I'm working full-time, and I've a good income from textbook royalties my father was kind enough to will me when he died, so I can afford to stop working while I write it. And my mother, who lives in the flat below me, is also very good with children, in spite of her academic bent and fascination with figures.'

His companion turned and stared at him, then shook her head, her blue eyes so puzzled he wanted to take her in his arms right then and there and never let her go.

'I couldn't actually have the babies, you'd have to do that,' he added, and the puzzled expression turned to wariness, and then suspicion.

'What babies would I have to have?' she demanded, and her tone of voice, the tension he could see in her body, told him instinct had betrayed him.

He'd got it wrong.

'Our babies?' he said hopefully. 'I'd stay home to care for them. You could keep working. Only it's anatomically impossible for me to—'

'I know what it's anatomically impossible for you to do, William,' she said. 'In fact I can think of a number of things that would fit under that heading, including some I'd like to suggest to you right now.'

And with that she ran on, leaving him on a path in the middle of Regent's Park, with an inner emptiness he suspected might never go away.

Perhaps if he let her cool down a bit.

Gave her time.

Had another go tomorrow.

He made his way disconsolately back to the hospital, then, realising tomorrow was too far away, he started searching through the likely places she might be. Coffee shop. Canteen. General Medical. The mess.

He caught up with her in the oncology ward at two for the latest episode in the daily drama. He and four patient-reporters, two patient-cameramen, a reporter, cameraman and sound man from the BBC, several nurses and ancillary staff who wanted to get on TV, a ward full of over-excited bald children, and a six-foot rabbit.

'Not a good time to talk?' he said, hoping for a smile at least.

What he got was a ferocious glare, eyes shooting scorn so hot it scorched his skin.

Not the best time, apparently!

The next day was even worse. After a sleepless night and a morning of anguished indecision, he arrived at the hospital at twelve in the vague hope she might at least agree to run with him. He couldn't find her anywhere, and when, in sheer desperation, he bleeped her and she called him back, the frosty voice informing him she was busy made him feel so cold and shivery he wondered if he might be sickening for something.

Chests! The rabbit was going to Chests today. If he got there first—

He made his way down to Dunwoody and bought a bunch of daffodils, then a second bunch as one looked a little paltry.

Back upstairs, he lay in wait outside the ward. After what seemed like hours the camera crew arrived, a nurse, presumably from Orthopaedics, accompanying the two boys. They set themselves up in the lift foyer so they'd get a clear shot of the rabbit when the lift doors opened.

William stood a little to one side, but close enough to thrust the flowers at Prue as she appeared. The presence of the 'camera crew' made it awkward, but a man had to do what a man had to do. He just hoped the camera would be focussed on the rabbit.

The bell pinged, the rabbit hopped out, waved to the camera, then turned to William, who was peering disconsolately into the empty lift.

'For me?' the rabbit said in a high falsetto. 'Oh, you shouldn't have!'

He then seized the flowers, waved them at the camera and while William watched he ate the golden blooms, one by one, until all he had left in his over-large paws was a bunch of sticky stalks.

The noise from the ward told William the children had thought this impromptu picnic riotously funny, *and* reminded him that the cameras were rolling. A televised attack on a cheerful Easter Bunny who'd become a hospital hero might not go down well with either patients or staff.

Curbing his murderous feelings, and contenting himself with a growl of rage at the rabbit, he stormed into the lift and pressed the down button.

He left a note on Prue's windshield suggesting dinner,

asking her to call him, carefully writing down his phone number. Then, certain she'd ignore the note, he drove not home, but to her place, where he found a parking space on the opposite side of the square, locked his car, and walked back towards her building.

She'd have to come home eventually. He'd sit on the steps.

'I'm used to people sleeping in doorways in central London now, but out here in the suburbs! And on our own steps? Really!'

The disgust in the voice penetrated his dream, and he woke with a start, to find himself cold, damp and uncomfortable, slumped against one of the pillars of the portico of Prue's building. The front door was just closing, but his memory of the voice told him it wasn't Prue who'd entered.

He held his watch so a street lamp shone on it and groaned when he saw the time. He'd taken a walk around the square at eight, then decided to sit down, and rest his back against the pillar.

That was two hours ago! Two hours in which he'd fallen asleep and his muscles had knotted while the pillar had pressed bruises into his flesh. Next time he saw someone living rough he'd be more understanding.

He climbed stiffly to his feet and walked around the square again. No sign of her car, so she hadn't walked past him while he'd slept.

She could have gone to stay with friends, he realised. She was on call for the next two days, but not required to be at the hospital unless she was needed. And if she had days off after that, she might not be home all week.

The prospect of a week spent sleeping on her doorstep was not at all appealing so he walked glumly back to his car, and drove home.

Lights were on in his mother's flat, and as he unlocked the front door he decided he'd call in and see her, sit with her a while, perhaps talk to her about this man-woman business at which he was proving so inept.

But as he drew closer to her door he heard her laughter and knew she must be entertaining. He could hardly arrive in his rumpled track suit and expect a heart-to-heart if she had company!

Disproportionately disappointed that he couldn't share his pain with someone, he headed up the stairs instead, muttering curses on all women—and men's inability to fathom them.

He tossed fitfully through another night, considered phoning Prue then decided, whether she'd been working or playing the previous evening, she certainly wouldn't welcome being woken too early. He'd have to bide his time— try again this afternoon. Surely she wouldn't trust the rabbit to find the eggs without being there herself.

The image of the rabbit popping flowers into his silly mouth made him want to grind his teeth in frustration.

Finally, fed up with his own company, he headed downstairs. He wouldn't make a fool of himself by telling his mother about Prue, but he could do with some TLC, and wasn't that what mothers were for?

He tapped out his usual two-three rhythm, then opened the door. Voices from the conservatory out the back suggested she was listening to the radio while she poked around amongst her plants or had a leisurely read of the paper.

'You there, Ma?' he called, and the radio went off.

Well, the voices stopped.

'Through here, dear,' his mother called.

As if he couldn't guess.

He walked through the gracious living room, the dining nook, and into the kitchen.

'Is the coffee-pot out there? Should I bring a cup?'

The conservatory was off the main bedroom of the flat,

a strange configuration due to the fact the bedroom, and the smaller one alongside it, had originally been a large reception room when the flats had been one house. It had another entrance off the back porch, and William paused there as he waited for a reply.

'No, dear, just come through,' his mother said, and as he stepped from the coolness of the outdoors to the warm humidity of the conservatory she added, 'I'll make fresh coffee for you. It's awful once it goes cold.'

And walked past him to the kitchen.

'Well, so much for her company!' he muttered to himself.

Then he was startled when a voice he'd been hearing in his restless dreams said, 'I think she was being discreet.'

He peered around the fecund greenery of a ginger plant, and there, sitting calmly at the little wrought-iron table at which he and his mother often shared a weekend breakfast, was the cause of all his confusion.

'What are you doing here?' he demanded, anger at her seeming so unconcerned vying with delight at seeing her again.

'Your mother found me on the doorstep and took pity on me.'

She had the hide to smile at him. One of those glimmering little smiles that made her eyes seem very bright and her freckles dance across her nose.

'Almost literally,' she continued. 'Once I had your phone number, I found your address in the phone book. I'd been rude—especially eating the flowers like that—'

'*You* ate my flowers? *You* were in the rabbit suit. No wonder I couldn't find you anywhere!'

At least she had the grace to look ashamed.

'You frightened me,' she said. 'Going on and on about staying home and having babies. We barely know each other. I've made one mistake—seen my mother make a half a dozen—I panicked, William. Couldn't handle it.'

'You didn't have to eat the flowers!' he growled, not certain where any of this was going, or if he should feel glad—which he did—or worried—which he also did.

'I didn't actually eat them, you know,' she told him. 'Just kind of plucked the tops off and shoved them down the mouth hole in the suit. It wasn't easy because that's where you look out from inside—through the mouth, not the eyes. Did you know that?'

William sighed.

Somehow, when he'd imagined meeting up with Prue again—eventually—the conversation hadn't been about the dynamics of seeing out of a rabbit suit.

'I'm sorry,' she said, apparently thinking his sigh was connected with the flowers. 'It completely threw me, seeing you standing there with the flowers in your hand.'

'So you ate them—or pulled off all their heads which I think is even worse. I mean, if you'd been hungry—'

He realised how ridiculous this conversation was and stopped.

'I think they might be poisonous so even if I was hungry…I mean that sticky sap. Ugh!'

He had to take control here! Get back on track.

But what track?

He held up his hands.

'That's it—that's enough. No more talk of rabbits or flowers. What's more to the point is what you're doing in my mother's conservatory. And don't give me that "found me on the doorstep" tale.'

Although if she'd gone home last night, wouldn't she have found him on her doorstep?

He looked into her face, and saw the smile flirting around her lips.

'To tell the truth, I didn't mean to stay. When you

weren't at home, didn't answer your bell, I was going to leave. Your mother came home from a walk at that moment and she said you probably wouldn't be long because you had absolutely no social life and why didn't I come in and wait.'

He'd speak to his mother later about her allegations but right now what had happened last night didn't quite explain—

'We had a glass of wine,' Prue added, 'then another. I knew I wasn't on call, so a third didn't seem like a bad idea, except it meant I couldn't drive home and then your mother said—'

'Stay the night!' He could hear his mother saying it.

'Well, yes,' Prue told him, a little flush of colour turning her cheeks the most delightful pink. 'I hope you don't mind, don't feel I was intruding. She was so kind. I mean, I told her we were just friends and that we'd had a misunderstanding and I wanted to clear it up, so she doesn't think…I mean, I don't think I gave her the impression it was anything more than that…'

The blue eyes looked so wary he wanted to assure her everything was all right—that he couldn't give a hoot what she had or hadn't told his mother. But he'd suffered the tortures of the damned over the past twenty-four hours and he wasn't going to let her off so lightly.

'You lied to my mother?' he said, colouring the words with total disbelief. 'Told her there was nothing between us? What about that kiss? Would you call that nothing?' As her eyes widened he realised he couldn't take it further, though he did add, 'And as for the icing!' as he stepped towards her and knelt in the soft sawdust mulch that covered the floor of the conservatory.

He took her hands and held them both in his, and looked up into her face.

'I did it all the wrong way around,' he admitted to her.

'It was the bells that threw me. What I was trying to say in the park was that it was safe for you to explore this thing between us further. That you need have no fears, if we took it further and did decide to get married, that I'd expect or even want you to give up your career. I wanted you to know I'd do the staying home, if you decided you wanted children—if we decided. I wanted you to feel secure. To know that it was safe to fall in love, if that's the way things happened, because love should be a bonus, not a penalty. Something special that adds an extra lustre to our lives, rather than a burden that brings more worries in its wake.'

He kept both her hands in one of his, and reached up with his free one to touch her cheek. 'Love's the bells and lights and whistles at the party, but it's also being there for each other. And I wanted you to know I'd always be there for you. With you all the way, Prue Valentine. 'Til death do us part.'

'Well, I'd say amen to that.' His mother's voice startled him to his feet. 'But don't rush the girl. I know you were so slow as to be almost comatose in courting Isobel. Fortunately she found someone who did want to commit to marriage, because she was never right for you, nor you for her, and deep down I think you knew that. Prue's different. She needs time.'

And now *his* mother had the hide to smile at Prue. The full female conspiracy in action.

'How much time?' he said, turning from the betrayal of his maternal relative to the woman who sat between them, gazing up at him with a bemused smile on her face.

'Eight years?' she said, then her smile turned to laughter and she stood up and flung herself into his arms.

'Or if that's too long, how about a week, or a day, or an hour, or a minute?' she said, hugging him as if she'd never let him go. Then she pulled away far enough to look into his eyes. 'It wouldn't matter how long I asked for, you wouldn't give it to me. You'd nag and carp and bulldoze over any objections until I gave in for some peace and quiet.'

He was about to argue, but as his mother was making her way out of the conservatory again, her shoulders shaking as if she was chuckling to herself, he decided there were better things to do with his lips than arguing, and he kissed the woman in his arms instead.

'We *do* need to get to know each other,' Prue said soberly. It was a long time later, and removing herself from his arms was proving very difficult. 'I mean, it's been less than three weeks since you caught me sleeping on the therapy table.'

'You can take as long as you like,' William told her. 'Because getting to know each other entails spending as much time as possible together and I can't think of a nicer fate. In fact, I'd like to think we're going to spend the rest of our lives getting to know each other.'

He kissed her nose, and then her eyelids, and Prue snuggled against his body. She was going to enjoy getting to know William. Enjoy the new sensations his kisses were generating, the fizz of excitement in her body whenever he was near her.

She raised her head and pressed her mouth to his, letting her kiss tell him all he needed to know.

'I've got some cake if you'd like it with your coffee.' Mrs Alexander's voice broke them apart. 'Chocolate, it is, with lovely thick icing.'

Which broke Prue up completely, and she collapsed against William's chest, laughing uncontrollably.

Yes, she was certainly going to enjoy getting to know him for the rest of her life. Especially getting to know about the icing.

Tender Romance™
6 brand new titles each month
...love affairs
that last a lifetime
Available on subscription every month
from the Reader Service™
GEN/02/RS2